God of the Brooks

Bruce Hamilton

God of the Brooks: A Story of Extreme Survival in Alaska

Bruce Hamilton
© 2017 Bruce Hamilton
All rights reserved

To Dad, who taught me how to
fish and how to pray. In that order.

Preface

Alaska has been my home since I was nine. The vast majority of my memories were formed in this great land. For a long time, I have wanted to share my experiences and adventures by way of writing.

This novel allows me to do that. Other than the plane crash that initiates the survival saga, most of the things that happen to my character in the storyline have happened to me here in the far north. To be sure, these events took place over a period of many years. Yet, many of them I have personally experienced. The places spoken of are also real and can be found on the USGS maps that are included.

The charging griz, the natural hot springs, the confrontation by the native man and his boy for trespassing and most of the adventures in between have all been a part of my personal journey

My goal in writing this book is that by the time a person finishes the story, he or she will know more about physical and spiritual survival, more about Alaska, the aurora, the Creator and His creation than ever before.

The pictures and video help bring this book to life. I encourage every reader to go to my website, www.godofthebrooks.com, and enjoy the visuals provided. It will be updated on a continual basis.

Some illustrations are from my personal collection while others are either used by permission or are in the public domain.

The website includes valuable information about visiting Alaska as well as a means to contact me.

If you have a suggestion, an observation, a corrective word, or a question about anything in the book, I would love to hear from you.

If you desire spiritual guidance, helping people is one of my great passions. Please contact me.

Enjoy!

Bruce Hamilton
Fairbanks, Alaska

TABLE OF CONTENTS

— **Important Note** —

For videos, maps, photos and background
information that will enhance your reading
experience, please utilize the website:
www.godofthebrooks.com

— 1 —
THE CRASH

I knew the griz was gonna charge. I'd been bluff-charged by enough bears to know this beast wasn't bluffing. The breeze, once friendly, had betrayed my presence. As soon as he caught my scent, he emerged from the brush popping his teeth, slobbering profusely and pouncing up and down on his freshly killed moose. As impressive as this display was, I knew that once he pinpointed my location, the real show would begin.

Strangely, I was unafraid. Instead, a mixture of anger and guilt swept over me: anger, because just a few weeks ago, my best huntin' buddy had died on the mountain; and guilt, because I too should've died. But I didn't. And in this moment, it seemed as though the only thing between me and home was this insane animal.

Refusing to become bear scat, I lifted my .454 Casull hand cannon. The movement, though slight, gave me away. He spotted the motion, leapt over the moose carcass and came at me full tilt. Even though this animal probably weighed close to a thousand pounds, he came with haste. Grizzlies can outrun the fastest racehorse the first one hundred yards.

Every time his front paws hit the tundra he blew—"Shoo!" "Shoo!" "Shoo!" "Shoo!" He sounded like a steam engine locomotive and looked as big. Every jump brought him twenty feet closer, so I had just seconds to aim, exhale, and pull that trigger. If my first shot didn't count, the moose would be his entrée. I'd be his dessert.

I've heard it said that when someone's about to die, his entire life flashes before him. Well, I got cheated because all I saw was the last three weeks.

The adventure began on a September Monday morning in my hometown of Fairbanks, Alaska. We loaded our food and gear into Les's Cessna 185, and while taxiing the plane to the south end of the runway, Les called FAA weather. The report crackled in our headphones: "Brooks Range: scattered clouds, ceiling—8,000 feet, visibility—2 miles, winds—west/northwest at 10 knots, possible showers mixed with snow, possible IFR conditions by tomorrow."

"Let's get while the gettin's good," Les said with his usual chuckle.

Then he pushed the throttle, and we were airborne. We headed north, looking down on the campus of the University of Alaska-Fairbanks. Turning slightly west, we were soon flying over Minto Flats. Seeing the many sloughs and lakes below brought to mind my first fishing adventure in Alaska. I was just a boy, nine years old. My dad had hired a floatplane operator to put us on one of the hottest fishing lakes in the interior. A day later we had so many giant northern pike that the pilot complained about possibly exceeding the maximum weight limits of his plane. As a boy, I had no clue what he was talking about, nor did I care. I was wide-eyed all the way home. I'd never seen so many huge fish. "That's a great memory," I whispered, smiling.

About thirty minutes later, the mighty Yukon River came into view. More hunting and fishing memories came to mind. I had hunted this famous drainage so often that it felt as if I was surveying my own backyard. The Yukon River divides Alaska completely in half, flowing northwest out of Canada and then west across Alaska. It looked big, even from four thousand feet.

The fall colors were astounding. The golden leaves of the paper birch contrasted with the dark green spruce. The tiny but countless blueberry bushes added a breathtaking splash of red for miles around. Occasionally, the landscape was punctuated by on old mining cabin, a homestead, or a native village. This was familiar territory. These were the things I was used to. This was my comfort zone. I felt blessed to have lived in this great state for over forty years.

Les and I had anticipated good flying weather all the way through the Brooks Range. As was our habit, we checked in with the weatherman again upon landing at Cold Foot. Cold Foot is the northern-most truck stop in the world, located at milepost 275 of the Dalton Highway. Because it was about the halfway point to our hunting area and because it had a nice airstrip, it had become our traditional refueling stop over the years. Of course, it didn't hurt a bit that they served up some great food in their café. We made it a point to be there by noon.

The forecast we had been given before leaving Fairbanks held true and had even improved a bit by the time we finished lunch at Cold Foot. The flight thus far had been exceptionally beautiful, and we were looking forward to getting airborne again. If only we had known that things were about to change— dramatically!

Our desire was to hunt the Killik and Colville Rivers, north of the Brooks Range. To access these game-rich drainages, we had decided to take a different route and, by so doing, scout new territory. Our plan was to fly about a thousand feet "off the deck" of the Alatna River, as Les put it, all the way through the pass, then on to the Killik and Colville.

By the time we got to the Brooks Range, however, the weather conditions had deteriorated. Soon the red and white Cessna was being tossed around like a mosquito in a hurricane. Les made another of his famous statements: "The weather man lied again." Only this time, he didn't chuckle.

We decided to climb our way out of the storm. I glanced at the altimeter and noticed that we were steadily gaining altitude. Ice pelted the aircraft. Massive clouds surrounded us. Visibility quickly diminished. Les and I had flown through tough conditions before, but never like this. Several tense minutes went by, and then we saw what appeared to be blue skies in the pass ahead. We even got a brief glimpse of sunlight. However, like bears being drawn to deadly bait, we were only lured deeper into the storm. About the time we thought it couldn't get any worse, it did. I expressed my fears, and Les quickly nodded his head in agreement.

We were at eight thousand feet and climbing. Nervously, I watched ice forming on the edges of the wings. I knew this could get deadly if the weight of the ice became more than the Cessna could handle. I worried even more when Les, with wrinkled brow, kept looking out his side window and mumbling under his breath. I'm sure he was calculating . . . and praying.

Then, as if on cue, the plane began shaking. One look at Les's face and I was scared enough to pray—out loud. He wasn't a man of fear, but fear is what I saw. I knew just enough to understand what was wrong. The weight of the ice had started to exceed the limits of the

11

aircraft. Suddenly, it banked sharply to the left.

"Are we turning around?" I shouted above the noise of the storm and engine.

"No!" he shouted in reply.

"I'm going to circle upward and try to get above this mess!"

He immediately reached for the throttle. I could tell the 185 was losing power. In response, Les gave her all she had. With strained voice he cried, "Lord, I need you now!"

We were completely helpless, at the mercy of God and the storm.

Then, out of nowhere, a plateau appeared in front of us. It was littered with boulders and was, at best, two hundred feet long. Les quickly cut the power and lowered the flaps. We hit—hard!

That was the last thing I remember until I heard someone moaning. It was me. I was trying to say "cold," but my mouth could not form the word. My body was wracked with pain. I was in and out of consciousness. For how long, I do not know.

All was dark when I next awoke. This time, I gained just enough consciousness to realize that Les was dead. Though I could not see him, I sensed it. I could hear death in the silence. There was no breathing, no moaning, and no movement from the pilot's side of the plane—just darkness . . . and silence . . . and cold. My thoughts were disjointed: "Why aren't we . . . why no . . . heat . . . no flying?" I struggled to think in sentences. "Thirsty . . . my leg . . . my head . . . the pain . . . thirsty . . . somebody help . . ."

I was hanging nearly upside down. The aircraft must've flipped upon hitting the rocks. I struggled to release the seat belt. Half falling, half rolling towards Les, I felt his claylike, lifeless body underneath. He was already stiffening.

In the darkness, I struggled and pushed my way through our gear and the mangled fuselage. Pain shot up and down my left leg. I screamed. The involuntary, raspy noise startled me. As consciousness increased, so did the pain, this time, in my abdomen and head. I could tell my nose was broken. My face was caked with blood. I could hardly open my mouth or breathe. More broken sentences punctuated my brain: "Thirsty . . . dry . . . throat . . . dry . . . so cold . . . oh . . . the pain!"

When I next regained consciousness, it was daylight. Shivering severely, I longed for warmth. If the injuries sustained in the crash didn't kill me, hypothermia would. I knew very well the dangers of hypothermia; after all, more outdoorsmen in Alaska meet their demise as a result of severe body heat loss than from any other cause. Yet, ironically, the cold had probably saved my life by slowing the loss of blood.

I forced my way further into the back of the wreckage, found a military mummy bag and crawled in. I then unzipped a gear bag, found a bottle of water, and drank. With trembling hand, I poured a little water on my face. The layer of blood loosened a bit, but it was so thick that I gave up and lay there, moaning, too weak to cry.

Sometime during the night, my head began to clear and I started to piece together what had happened. In the dense clouds and ice storm, Les must've tried to climb out of the weather by circling the plane upwards. The wings must have collected too much ice, robbing the aircraft of its ability to fly. Then I vaguely recalled an attempt to crash land. It must've been more crash than land because my best hunting buddy was dead, and here I was dying . . . alone . . . on this massive rock.

In the darkness, I was weak, wounded, and helpless. Finally, I was able to cry. I wept long and loud. I wailed for my friend and for the grief I knew his family must endure. I cried for my family. I cried in physical pain. I cried in emotional and spiritual pain. My sobs became prayers. I cried out to the Lord. I repented of sin, begged for mercy, and gave thanks for grace. I worshipped Him in earnest for the first time in years. I knew the Lord in a personal way but had been living far from Him for a long while. No more. If I survived this horrific event, I promised God my willing obedience. I knew in that moment, my life was changed.

Immediately a great peace came over me. Bible verses flooded my mind. Some I had memorized as a child; others I had read only once or twice. I quoted Psalm 23 in a raspy whisper. The entire eighth chapter of Romans came to me so clearly that it seemed like someone was reading it aloud. I slept, prayed, and wiped the tears away throughout the night.

At daybreak, this conflicting experience continued. One moment it seemed as if God had wrapped His arms around me; then, in the next, my heart and mind would plummet to the depths of fear and despair. Heaven and the presence of the Lord had never seemed so real, yet tragedy and death had never been so near. My body was weak and wracked with pain, yet, at times, I felt immense joy and a great calm in my soul. This experience was a powerful contradiction. With tears carving trails down my bloodstained face, I caught myself smiling; then I crawled deeper into the mummy bag and slept.

Sometime later I awoke, drank more water, and spent at least an hour washing my face. I was assaulted by intense hunger. Rummaging through shredded aluminum and broken glass, I found a package of beef sticks and some cheese. The meager fare strengthened my body and my mind, but the pain in my abdomen and leg increased.

It was then that I recalled Les's personal medicine bag. He had undergone rotator cuff surgery a few months back and had brought some prescription pain meds just in case. They were like gold to me. Good or bad, wise or unwise, I took them liberally and soon lost track of time. My days were filled with pills, sleep, water, and food. The minutes, hours, and days became irrelevant. Thanks to the pills, so did the pain. Mission accomplished—at least temporarily.

As my condition improved, I was able to deal with reality and ascertain the situation in which I found myself. In one brief moment, my world had shrunk from the expanse of the Brooks Range to the span of my outstretched arms. I was a prisoner to the Alaskan wilderness, stranded on top of a huge rock, a stone so massive that it would be considered a mountain by "lower forty-eight" standards. I was at the mercy of God and the elements. To survive would require every bit of knowledge I owned, every ounce of prudence I possessed, and every drop of strength I could regain. "Lord, help me . . ." I mumbled, and fell back asleep.

It was several days before I could exit the wreckage. During that time, I had urinated in empty water bottles. Where to defecate had not been a problem because of one simple fact: I couldn't. I was extremely constipated. It could very well have been a side effect of the pain meds. But it could also be the result of internal injury. That possibility concerned me most. If I had blockage somewhere in my intestines, it would eventually kill me. I hoped and prayed it was simply a side effect of the meds.

Late one night, I decided I had gained enough strength to examine my wounds. I waited for sunlight to fall into the aluminum casket in which I lay and then painfully struggled to undress. My left leg was still swollen just above the knee, so it took great effort and some cutting to remove my jeans. They were stiff with dried blood. Once exposed, the wound was sickening to look at. It was more than a cut. It was a substantial gash and was grossly discolored around the perimeter. Obviously, I had been thrust forward with tremendous force, and my leg had been sliced open by something on my left. It didn't take long to find the culprit. The GPS was in two pieces, hanging in the twisted bracket with dried blood and a piece of my jeans stuck to it.

I knew there was a first-aid kit somewhere, but hand sanitizer was all I could find. Gingerly, I bathed the gash. The alcohol stung immensely, resulting in yet another involuntary scream. Once the sanitizer dried, I cut a clean t-shirt into strips and used them as bandages. I then put on clean long johns and socks and wearily crawled into my sleeping bag—cold, fatigued, and afraid.

After resting and before nightfall, I examined my stomach and lower abdomen. The multicolored bruising from the seat belt was horrific and made me nauseated. My abdomen was black and blue and green. I stared at it, wide-eyed, for just a few seconds; then I lowered my shirt and attempted to combat fearful imaginations with happy thoughts. The last thing I needed was to add stress to my already troubled soul. But alas, my mind refused to abandon reality. It kept returning to my injuries, especially the ones not visible. Those are the ones that could kill me.

As darkness fell, I prayed:

"Lord, Thy will be done in earth . . . on this rock . . . as it is in heaven. Thy will be done . . . Thy will be done . . ."

As that phrase echoed in my mind, I began to level with God:

"Lord, why is it I pray only when I'm desperate or afraid? Why do I seek Your face only when I need or want something? It's so self-serving, so proud. But that's me, Lord. That's who I've been for a long, long time—absorbed with myself instead of You. Forgive me."

A few minutes passed and I continued:

"Please teach me the *communion* of prayer that I might know more than just the *urgency* of prayer. Teach me the joy of yielding to Your will every moment, not just when I'm in need of Your help."

I lay there that night ruminating about my lack of sincere fellowship with God. I soon found myself as concerned about my *spiritual* condition as I was about my *physical* condition.

"That's a good thing." I proclaimed.

"I guess nothing causes a man to inventory his life more than a face-to-face encounter with death."

As repentance swept across my heart and tears ran down my face, I fell asleep under the night sky of the Brooks.

"This is no way to start the day," I said hoarsely as I painfully peeled more dried blood from my face. The process was, again, excruciating. It quickly drained me of what little energy sleep had provided. I slumped against the fuselage, panting. Desperate, I rummaged through the gear and found a small bottle of lotion, which greatly aided in removing the remaining scabs from my face and, finally, my arms.

As my condition slowly improved, my desire to exit the wreckage increased. I felt trapped, even claustrophobic. I determined to exit the fuselage as soon as possible. In my mind, it had morphed from a blessing to a curse. To be thinking that way indicated I was making progress. For the first time in a while, I felt excited.

However, I had a crucial decision to make: Do I leave the crash site completely, or stay nearby, hoping to be rescued? Since the plane was practically upside down and the tail section demolished, it was very likely that the Emergency Locator Transmitter (ELT) had also been destroyed. Had it been sending a rescue signal, help would have arrived days earlier.

In addition (and to our shame) Les and I rarely told anyone where we were going when planning a moose or sheep hunt. Alaskans are funny that way. They'll tell you where they get their caribou, their fish, and maybe their black bear but ask about moose or sheep and the crickets start chirping. You get nothing, or worse, you get the sourdough[1] answer: "Birch Creek."

All sourdoughs know there are about a hundred "Birch Creeks" scattered across the state. Sometimes, snoopy inquirers get the hint. The naïve Cheechakoes[2] don't. Whenever a Cheechako asks, "Where'd you get that big moose?" my huntin' buddies and I respond with "Birch Creek" or "We got 'em on the Wish-You-Knew River."

That seemed humorous at the time. However, I greatly wished we had told at least our families of our flight plan or destination. The reality was, we had not. Therefore, my chances of being found by Civil Air Patrol or by military search and rescue were about zero. In spite of that, if I were prepared to light a signal fire and could do so quickly, I might be able to draw the attention of an aircraft passing over. This and the need to take inventory of my supplies and situation made me more determined to exit the aircraft soon.

Since the crash, I had not even ventured outside to use the latrine. In addition, I had had no bowel movement. This, along with the persistent pain in my lower abdomen still very much concerned me. Internal bleeding or intestinal blockage could easily make this mountain my final resting place. If I were to die, I at least wanted my body found so that my family could have closure. Many have perished in arctic plane crashes whose bodies were never recovered. That thought pushed me over the edge, literally.

"I've got to escape this mountain!"

That night, I formulated my plan, step by step:

(1) Exit the aircraft first thing in the morning.

(2) Inventory my supplies, including first-aid materials and medications. (I desperately needed more pain meds and a laxative)

(3) Gather flammable material for a signal fire in case I heard any aircraft overhead.

---

[1] Seasoned Alaskan

[2] A "Cheechako" is what the Alaskan natives used to call someone new to Alaska. During the early gold rush days, it seemed to them that everyone coming to Alaska was from Chicago. They pronounced the word *Chicago* like "Cheechako." So that became the name for anyone new to the area.

(4) Search for a way to descend the mountain.

(5) Clear the fuselage of any broken or unnecessary items.

(6) Cover my damaged shelter with a bright blue tarp.

Every Alaskan owns at least three tarps, almost always blue. Even our state flag resembles a blue tarp with the exception that the flag has "eight stars of gold." A giant blue tarp is considered a must by most Alaskan outdoorsmen, and Les and I were no exception. I knew there were at least two on board, and they would be extremely useful. The bright color would serve as a signal to other aircraft, and the plastic material would weatherproof my temporary sleeping quarters.

I awoke before daylight and couldn't wait any longer. Using my flashlight, I surveyed the area closest to me. The pilot's door was completely missing, but Les's body, still hanging by the seatbelt, blocked that exit. I could have struggled past him, but I did not want to climb over or around his corpse. There was a lot of dried blood underneath his head. His face was not recognizable. Only the low temperatures had kept him from decomposing on what I assumed was the sixth or seventh day since the crash. Being in the same confined area with the lifeless body of my friend was extremely disturbing, so I turned my gaze to the other side of the plane.

The copilot's door was mangled and blocked inside by gear that had been thrown forward. The cargo door was nearest to me and though damaged, appeared to be my most likely exit. Even though it was a much smaller opening than the others, I knew I could fit through it.

I forced it completely open with my right leg and crawled out, feet first. As soon as I put pressure on my left leg, I collapsed, gasping in pain. Immediately the cold air sliced through me like a fillet knife! Having been protected in the shelter of the plane, I was completely caught off guard by the extreme, flesh-freezing wind. Shaking uncontrollably, I struggled back inside and felt quite defeated.

All of my injuries revived. The pain pounded like a dozen hammers on my head, face, abdomen, and leg. Without rising, I began reaching for and opening every bag, looking for pills. In my desperation, all I could find was a bottle of over-the-counter meds that brought little relief. After an hour or so, I fell asleep.

It was dark when I awoke, so I just lay there thinking—out loud. By mumbling my thoughts, I was able to brainstorm more effectively. I must've sounded like a crazy old sourdough. Nevertheless, it helped to converse with myself about what to do next:

"I need food, water, medicine, and more clothing before I step (or fall) outside this wreckage again."

Audibly moving down the checklist I queried, "What about your leg?"

Answer: "Do not put pressure on your left leg. Steady yourself against the fuselage."

Next question: "Why must you venture outside?"

Answer: "In order to study the crash site for position, elevation, combustible materials, and a possible escape route down the mountain."

"Why else?"

"So that I can remove any and all destroyed or unnecessary items from inside the aircraft, thereby creating more useable space."

The self-interrogation continued: "And?"

"To preserve my sanity."

"Then what?"

"I will inventory my condition and survival gear in preparation for the escape."

"And?"

"Leave me alone! I'm tired and hurt—and a little bit crazy right now!"

This schizoid-type conversation with myself actually helped me process my situation, which wasn't easy in my condition. I continued to use this self-interrogation style Q and A often throughout my recovery. I think it helped ward off loneliness as well.

By midafternoon of the next day, I was finally "on the outside looking in," so to speak. The wreckage was horrific. The plane had obviously hit the rocky surface hard on the pilot's side and then flipped. Material was scattered helter-skelter in every direction. Pieces of aluminum, the extra-large tundra tire from Les's side of the plane with the landing gear still attached, and a chunk of the prop were just a few of the items readily visible.

The wing on the pilot's side had been completely ripped off and was at least thirty feet behind the fuselage. The wing on the passenger's side was attached but mangled. The smell of 100-octane fuel still lingered.

The crash site was fairly level but fell away steeply on three sides, less than one hundred feet from where I stood. Was that chance or providence? It seemed impossible that I could be standing in the midst of such destruction, alive.

I whispered, "It had to have been the providence of God that spared my life. But why me? Why wasn't my friend spared, or why didn't both of us perish?" I concluded it was quite useless to try to figure all that out right now. This wasn't a time for philosophical queries or deep religious questions. I had work to do.

— 2 —
THE CLIFF

Careful not to put any pressure on my injured leg, I slowly pulled our hunting gear from the plane: two broken lanterns, shattered plastic containers, tarps, air mats, a crushed two-burner stove, groceries, camp chairs, and more. Everything was either sideways or an upside-down mess. I was basically clearing the ceiling—which had become the floor—of the aircraft.

I then searched every bag and box and carefully placed all necessary items back inside. During the inventory process, I found several military MREs, or Meal Ready to Eat packets. Each one is a complete meal in itself. I had always appreciated the fact that Les preferred home-cooked meals on a hunt, as did I, so we rarely used the MREs. His cooking skills were actually quite good. "Bad weather may hamper good huntin'; but rain, snow, or shine, we're gonna eat mighty fine," he'd say with his characteristic deep chuckle. In spite of all the chef talk, we brought along half a dozen MREs just in case.

In the midst of my daydreaming, I suddenly recalled that every MRE contained a packet of instant coffee. Trembling with excitement, I cut through one of the heavy plastic packages and soon found two little packets labeled "Coffee—Medium Roast."

Finding a single burner stove and a bent but still useable sauce pan, I carefully moved away from any exposed aircraft fuel, lit a fire, melted snow, and started cooking coffee. In just minutes, I was sipping and savoring a much needed and, in my opinion, well-deserved cup of Java. I'd had nothing so rejuvenating in days! This was my first morale booster in quite a while. Discovering the prefab meals was a wonderful surprise that was only heightened by the packets of coffee. That night for the first time in several days, I ate heartily.

The sun was setting by the time I crawled back inside the fuselage. Having accomplished some of my goals, I felt a great sense of achievement but was completely exhausted. I was weak as a rag doll and hurting but encouraged by the new information I had gathered. It wasn't exactly good news, but at least I knew what challenges lay ahead. Or I thought I did.

Leaning back in the new tin and tarp motel, I once again began to think out loud:

"I have a limited amount of food, maybe enough for ten or twelve days, if I stretch it."

I leaned back, closed my eyes and continued:

"With snow all around, water is not an issue. Some items were destroyed in the crash. Yet many things survived, either intact or still useful. I have my knife, Les's hatchet, matches, a lighter, my .454 Casull handgun with cross-draw holster, and five rounds of ammo. I have 550 cord, blue tarps, a change of clothes, my hunting jacket, binoculars, daypack, meds, plastic bags, MREs, and my sleeping bag."

Could I get myself and all of these things off this mountain? I had to if I were to survive, recover, and possibly escape or be rescued from this vast wilderness. Descending this rock plateau would be perilous even for someone in great condition. It would be ten times more difficult and dangerous for me.

Suddenly, I decided to be patient and remain here as long as possible. Each day I delayed would bring more healing and strength. I could rest, eat, drink, and listen for any passing aircraft. At first light, I would prepare my signal fire and simply wait.

Within hours, however, that plan was vetoed quickly and violently. In the middle of the night, the storm came. It came suddenly and with a great noise. It sounded like an eighteen-wheeler barreling down upon me. My eyes flew open. Why did I not anticipate this? This is exactly the kind of weather for which these mountains are famous. Now, "this storm is gonna blow me right off the edge of nowhere!" was my spoken fear. Why didn't I at least tie the main part of the aircraft down? Why did I leave so much gear outside?

With each powerful gust of wind, my mangled aluminum shelter was lifted from the rocks and almost hurled off the cliff. The tarps I had used to cover the plane clapped like thunder. I could tell one of them had been partially ripped from the tie downs and was being shredded. I was in agony, knowing many supplies were going to be swept away, forever gone.

For brief periods, the storm would tease me with a temporary calm, but within minutes, it would return more furious and life threatening than before. I could hear it coming a few seconds before it slammed against my precarious perch. I was completely at the mercy of the elements, and they were without mercy.

At one point, in between onslaughts, I crawled outside, flashlight in my mouth, rescued some gear and barely made it back inside before the next wave hit. It was painful and frightening, but I had to do it. After three forays into the teeth of the storm, I could endure no more. All night I prayed: "Lord, I believe you spared my life in the crash for a reason; please save me from the jaws of death once again!" Little did I realize how often in the days to come I would pray that prayer.

Before daybreak, the storm subsided and I slept. Upon waking, I felt drained, physically and emotionally, from the duress of the storm. Nevertheless, I crawled outside for just a few minutes to relieve myself and survey the area. The plateau was as clean as if someone had swept it with a giant broom. The detached wing was gone as was every item not brought inside. Nothing but boulders and, thankfully, the fuselage, remained. I limped back to the plane and spent the remainder of the day eating, drinking, sleeping, and, of course, revising my plans.

I knew I could not risk another mountain storm like that. Though weak and wounded, I must figure out a way to escape this precarious rock. I decided to venture further from the shelter the next morning. It should be doable because there wasn't much surface area to explore. I could hobble no more than one hundred feet in any direction before encountering empty space. That feature alone minimized the physical demands that my little reconnaissance mission would require.

There had to be a way down this mountain. It would require the use of a rope, of that I was sure. No matter. I'd rather risk my life escaping this exposed mountain shelf than chance being blown overboard by the next horrific storm. I must be proactive. I was convinced that the next storm would be fatal.

At daybreak, I consumed an MRE and, like a very old bear coming out of its den, stiffly emerged from the plane. It was a clear day and the wind had died, so I assembled material for a signal fire. A cup of gasoline and a shredded tundra tire was about all I could scavenge after the storm. The gasoline would ignite quickly and the rubber from the tire would create lots of black smoke. Everything was ready. I just needed to hear a plane. For now, it was my best hope of being rescued. With my ears tuned to the sky and my eyes focused on the surroundings, I set to work.

Favoring my left leg, I started toward the rear of the crash site looking for an escape route. After about fifty haltering paces I pronounced, "Nope, too steep." Limping around to the pilot's side, I saw that it too was a sheer drop-off. By the time I got to the passenger's side of the plateau, I had to rest. Flat on my back, I assessed my predicament:

"Well, if there's no way down this next edge, I may have to build a hang glider and fly down," I quipped, trying to reclaim my sense of humor.

After adding one more prayer to my ever-expanding collection, I limped over to the last precipice for a look:

"No way. This one's steeper than all the rest combined!"

It was as though someone had kicked me in the stomach. The hope that had been inside me slowly started melting. I sat down against the wreckage, put my hands over my face, and cried.

After a time of having a good, old-fashioned pity party, I felt strongly impressed to retrace my steps. Only this time, I determined that I would belly-crawl and peek further over each ledge. Slowly, I limped over, then dropped to all fours and crawled.

Eventually, an inch at a time, I slid my way to each precarious possibility. I began to sweat like I did when I proposed. I have always been afraid of heights, but desperation drove me over the edge—*literally*!

"Nope, another stinkin' three-thousand foot drop-off," I said with disgust. "Try again."

Reluctantly, I limped over to the cliff's edge behind the plane and lay down on my stomach. I absolutely dreaded the inevitable view.

First, just my eyebrows extended over the cliff and then… my forehead head…and eyes.

Finally, just to "go the extra mile," I somehow forced my neck and shoulders into empty space.

I had no sooner questioned my sanity when I saw what appeared to be a narrow ledge about one hundred feet below. Tucked into the mountainside, it appeared to be some sort of game trail. I had not spotted it before because it wasn't readily visible. I crawled back a safe distance and then limped back to my shelter.

I was trembling. Was it fear or excitement? "Both!" I answered, with a nervous grin.

Deep into the night I pondered that trail. It was more than likely used by Dall sheep. Only the sure-footed wild sheep and mountain goats ventured across terrain so dangerous. To be sure, bears and wolves climb far higher but would probably not attempt to navigate such a steep, rocky slope. So it had to be a sheep trail, and since Dall sheep must occasionally descend to the valley for water, I knew that if I could get to that trail, it should . . . it could . . . it *would* lead me off this mountain!

How much rope had Les brought on this trip? I decided to look for it tomorrow. I just didn't have the strength to search for it now.

"Be patient," I whispered. "Rest. You're going to need it to escape Death Mountain."

After an MRE breakfast and two cups of coffee, I began scouring the back of the fuselage with the help of the flashlight. Soon I spotted a coiled piece of rope. Of course, it just had to be as far back in the crushed tail section as possible. With a fully extended hiking pole, I managed to fish it out. It was 100' long and ½" in diameter. Hopefully, it would be long enough as well as strong enough to hold my 185 pounds. Even though the rope wasn't new, neither did it appear to be dry-rotted or worn.

The plane was too far away from the plateau's edge to use as an anchor, so I began searching the area. I spotted a large boulder fifteen to twenty feet from the precipice. I wrapped the rope securely around the rock several times and threw the line "overboard."

It fell short of my objective by at least thirty feet, partly due to my wrapping it around the boulder. Thirty feet would be a fatal drop for anyone, much less someone with multiple injuries. So I pulled the rope back up and added a long triple strand of 550 military parachute cord, a standard item in our hunting gear.

"That should do it," I said aloud as I tossed it over the cliff.

"With my six foot frame, that should give me enough length to reach the trail."

I carefully crawled to the edge once again and nervously confirmed my hope. The rope was dangling just a few feet above the path to freedom.

"I'll rest, organize, and pack for the next two days then I'll risk it all to get to the valley below."

I immediately prayed that, in the interim, no more storms would arise.

Finally, the big day arrived. By that time, I had meticulously filled my pack with the most essential survival items: matches, plastic lighter, three 12-ounce bottles of water and a plastic water bag, the last two MREs, several beef sticks, crackers, a one-pound block of cheese, a few candy bars, a hatchet, the remainder of the 550 cord, a small flashlight with extra batteries, my compact hunter's Bible, Les's skinning knife (his knife was of better quality than my own, and I wanted a keepsake that would remind me of my friend), a small pair of binoculars, a roll of flagging, my tin coffee mug, the bent sauce pan, a few sealable plastic bags, an extra set of clothes (including Les's spare long johns), two extra pairs of his wool socks, a soft wool hat, insulated hunting gloves, a small first-aid kit, and all remaining meds, especially the laxative, which was almost depleted but, thankfully, had been working quite well. I then wrapped a blue tarp around my sleeping bag and tied it on top of the daypack.[3]

My sleeping bag was more modern and lightweight than Les's army-issue mummy bag. The old government bags were filled with goose down and were heavy. In addition, if they got wet, they'd lose most of their insulating ability. The newer, lighter, civilian bags were filled with a man-made product that retained much of its loft even when damp.

---

[3] My pack was frameless. Les did not allow backpacks with frames in his plane. They tended to gouge the inside fabric.

I greatly regretted losing the GPS that had been destroyed in the crash, especially since my left leg had been the culprit. I looked at the maps we had brought with us. Unfortunately, they were all of our hunting areas north of the Brooks and would be of no use to me now.

So this was my stash. The combined weight of my earthly possessions was about forty-five pounds, give or take. These things would be all I had once I descended the mountain. I wished I could take more but felt I was already pushing the limit considering the precarious escape I was about to attempt.

Still weak from my injuries but full of adrenaline, I strapped the holster across my chest and snapped the pistol securely in place. I had no rifle. Typically, I did not bring a rifle on our hunts because my hobby was filming and producing amateur outdoor videos. Early in my filming career, I realized it was impractical to try to carry camera equipment and a rifle at the same time. The hands-free solution when mostly filming was the holster and handgun.

I had hunted with my big bore pistol before and had great confidence in it. One of the main reasons for purchasing that particular weapon was its versatility. With the .454, I could practice on small game using lighter bullets such as the .45 longs or I could use the much heavier 440-grain bullets for big game.

The Casull was made by Freedom Arms and held five rounds instead of the usual six because of the "beefed up" cylinder. The fine machine work on this baby was second to none and it was fully loaded! Unfortunately, I wasn't in the habit of bringing extra ammo since my primary focus was filming as opposed to hunting and fishing so, the five bullets in the cylinder were all I had.

I had considered taking Les's favorite rifle, a pre-'64, .375 hunting rifle, but sadly, it had been broken in the crash. I had found the rifle while sorting through the gear and discovered a major crack in the stock, just behind the trigger guard. When I removed the screw, the stock fell into two pieces. Even so, it would have made a great keepsake, but for survival purposes, it was useless.

Soon, the pistol was in place, and the pack was secured on my back by the straps that were tied across my chest.

After taking inventory one last time, I removed my hunting cap and prayed:

"Lord God of all creation, truly You are sovereign. My life is in Your hands. I trust in Your goodness, mercy, and grace. I believe You spared my life for a reason. Fulfill that purpose in me. Please protect me from my own impatience and from any foolish decisions. Please, Lord, allow me to escape this barren mountain and see my family once again. Amen."

Quite suddenly, a safety measure came to mind:

"Tie knots intermittently along the rope."

This I did. Then I made sure the line was fastened securely to the boulder. I tossed the rope over the edge. It fell about eight to ten feet short. I was sure it was due to the knots I had added. But I was six feet tall, and I figured a two- or three-foot drop wouldn't kill me.

"No more delays," I stated emphatically. "It's time to 'get while the gettin's good!'"

— 3 —
THE CONVALESCENCE

After using paper trash, gasoline, and pieces of aircraft tire to light a signal fire, I nervously crawled backwards. In vain, I had tried to remember how professional mountain climbers make a saddle with the rope in order to control their descent. Not only could I not duplicate the process, but I also didn't have enough rope. So I settled for running the rope behind the holster and holster harness. If nothing else, this would give me a little more control of my descent or at least provide me with an extra second or two to re-grip in an emergency. It was obvious the rope would slide through these weak barriers almost effortlessly. However, the knots would catch for a brief moment. Or so I hoped.

Just before dangling into the cold, arctic air, I grasped the first big knot and had just started backing over the edge when I thought the rock moved!

Did the rock move or was it my imagination?

Filled with fear, I quickly reversed my course and painstakingly dug a large, deep hole directly in front of the boulder so that if it did roll, it would fall into the depression. As far as insurance goes, it was slightly better than nothing.

Determined to "do or die," I nervously returned to the rope and, resisting the urge to look down, slid about two feet over the edge, then a couple more, and then more.

I was terrified, trembling like a frightened puppy. Before I knew it, I found myself dangling over the cliff. I reached for the rope with my right leg and wrapped it around the life-saving cord. Slowly and methodically, it slipped around my leg and through my hands. I was about one-third of the way down, with the rope digging deeply into my gloves when, shockingly, I fell!

Just as quickly, I was jerked to a stop. The knot to which I was clinging saved my life. The sudden jolt almost threw me off the line and into frozen space. In an instant, I was sweating, breathing heavily, and feeling very helpless. My heart rate rocketed. I could feel my pulse pounding in my throat. I literally felt death's icy breath on the back of my neck. My mind was racing. The boulder must've rolled or slid!

The hole I had dug and the knots I had been impressed to tie very likely had just saved my life. Were it not for those two precautions, I would've certainly plunged to my death.

"Thank you, Lord. Now, please help me. Please keep that rock in place. Please keep the line secure. Please have mercy on me!" I pled with my teeth clenched and eyes closed. Fighting panic, I continued further down wishing for, stretching for, feeling for the ground beneath. It took all my will power and then some just to keep calm. Finally, I reached the 550 cord and knew I was over two thirds of the way to safety.

"Just thirty more feet," I whispered, grimacing…"Just twenty more feet," I coached.

There were no knots in the parachute cord to help me, so I had to wrap it around my hands and let it slide through as I inched downward. The line was slicing into the gloves and pinching my fingers. The pain was excruciating. My hands and wrists were completely numb from lack of circulation. With about fifteen feet to go, my right glove got stuck in the line, and I had to continue, barehanded and bleeding. For a moment I was tempted to let go. Surely, there were only a few feet to go--just five or six, maybe?

"No!" I growled in pain.

"Persevere . . . to the ground!" I commanded, knowing my leg couldn't take anymore shock or injury. Gritting my teeth, sweating profusely, and with tears running down my face, I finally and literally reached "the end of my rope." I had no choice now but to "let go and let God," as they say.

Nervously, I ventured a peek. "Yes!"

I was just two or three feet shy of a smooth landing. With a quick prayer and dreading what I knew was coming, I let go of the cord and hit the ground.

Immediately I collapsed, in agony. My left leg was wet, probably with blood and my abdomen was in great pain. My hands were pulsating, bleeding, and completely numb.

I curled up like a baby in the fetal position and cried. Yet, it was not a cry of pain or fear or sorrow. I cried for joy. I had made it to the ledge below. I had escaped the plateau of death…I was alive and the good Lord willing, I'd soon be on my way and off this horrific mountain.

With pack still on and the rope still dangling above, I lay there quite some time. To the Bald Eagles circling above, I must've looked like a giant snail, fallen on its side.

My nerves and heart rate finally began to settle. The gallon of adrenaline that had been coursing through my veins started to subside. Slowly, the feeling returned to my hands and arms. Every part of my body was screaming for attention. It did not matter. I had time to recover.

"There's no hurry now," I whispered. So, I just lay there on my side and savored the warmth of sunshine and victory.

The late fall sky was a deep blue. The jagged gray and white mountain peaks contrasted strikingly against it. A few clouds were being hurried along by the winds aloft. The beautiful scene brought to mind how my life is moved along by the will of God.

"My life is but a vapor," I silently quoted while contemplating how fragile, how temporary this life is.

"Thank-you, God, for the promise of eternal heaven and a king- dom that will never pass away."

After quite some time, I rolled onto my stomach and then slowly, painfully, progressed to my hands and knees. Finally, I stood and leaned against the rocky cliff. It was time to take inventory and get moving. My head was pounding but I wasn't dizzy; my nose, still swollen a bit, was throbbing; my abdomen hurt but not to the degree it had a few days ago; my leg, now the most serious of my injuries, was swelling once again and throbbing with pain. It felt wet. I'm sure the flesh wound had been torn open by the sharp rocks during my descent. Blood was seeping through my jeans. My hands were stinging, the flesh, torn. With facial injuries that prob- ably included two black eyes, I must've looked like a Brooks Range Zombie. It did not matter. I was off the worst part of the mountain, alive and… almost kickin'.

I limped along the game trail until the sun disappeared. Still a long way from timber, I prepared to spend the night exposed on the mountainside. I set my gear down, removed my pants and washed my leg with the last of the hand sanitizer. It stung as though a dozen angry, kamikaze wasps had attacked my leg! I wished for a piece of wood to bite on like they did in the Old West during surgery.

Once the burning subsided, I wrapped the wound with a clean but rather primitive bandage made from strips of t-shirt. What little gauze there had been in the first-aid kit was long gone. Infection was my greatest concern. The area around the wound, just above the knee, was quite inflamed. If I could make it to the tree line tomorrow, I'd set up camp and focus exclusively on treating my leg. I must frequently and thoroughly clean the injury and give myself time to heal.

After an uncomfortable night, I ate, loaded up, and hobbled forward. It was barely light.

"I'd give a hundred bucks for a walking stick," I said aloud, and before my words echoed back to me, I gasped and drastically raised the offer. There, fifty feet in front of me, the trail turned deadly. It narrowed to no more than two feet wide with a thousand-foot drop on either side! Even though the drop wasn't straight down, it was so steep that were I to fall, I'd be ripped to shreds by hundreds of feet of shale.[4]

Just when things were looking up, I was instantly too afraid to look down. The extremely narrow trail was at least a mile long and descended sharply in front of me. It was as if I were looking across the narrow spine of Death Mountain.

"Will I ever escape this place?" I whispered in frustration.

Like a trapped animal, I searched for an alternate route. There was no other way. The only option was to return to the cliff, climb the rope and die at the crash site. For a second, I was tempted. However, after much prayer and making sure my load was perfectly balanced, I stepped forward.

"Don't look to the right; don't look to the left; just watch the path

---

[4] Shale is a very sharp rock formation common in Alaska. It has such an edge that the Alaska natives made knives and spear points with it thousands of years ago. It is similar to flint.

ahead," I chanted nervously.

The first step was the most frightening. Cautiously, I placed one foot in front of the other. There was no room for mistakes.

"Lord, guide me." I prayed, trembling. I had no sooner taken that first step when suddenly, a verse from the Bible came to mind. It was almost audible.

"This is the way, walk in it."

The scripture came so clearly and with such clarity that it startled me. I blinked back a few ill-timed tears and began walking with a confidence unknown to me before. Emotion welled up within as I recounted how that very same bible verse had been given by God to my mother during the midst of her deepest trial.

Her son, my brother Johnny, had been diagnosed with leukemia at just twelve years of age. One day, according to Mama, as she was returning to the hospital after a much-needed break, she saw a narrow footpath across the lawn and decided to take it. She told me that the very moment she stepped into the pathway, a verse of Scripture came to her mind: "This is the way, walk ye in it" [Isa. 30:21]. She said it was so clear, so suddenly clear, that it startled her and gave her great peace when peace was desperately needed.

"The Lord is most real to us in times of deepest need," she had said to me after retelling this story.

"Wow, what a comforting memory. Thank you, Lord. Thank you, Mama."

As I ventured forward, eyes focused on each next step, I couldn't help but notice fresh sheep tracks. It didn't surprise me. I was amazed, however, to see wolf scat with sheep hair mixed in it at this elevation.

After what seemed an agonizing hour, I chanced a glance straight ahead and was encouraged by my progress. This positive moment, however, produced a little too much confidence, and I peeked over the edge. Immediately, I regretted doing so. My heart rate quickened.

"That's a sure way to die if I ever saw one!" I exclaimed.

Quickly, I refocused on the path to avoid becoming dizzy and determined not to do that again.

Each step was a risk I had to take in order to make the journey home. Every move required intense concentration. The steep descent suddenly became much steeper and, of all things, narrower. As if that was not a great enough challenge for an injured man, the path became loose and unstable because of an increase in gravel. Just as I was trying to process these new challenges, I slipped and fell!

Had I not fallen backwards, the journey would've ended there. With head pounding, I steadied myself and slowly stood. I wished a thousand times that I had thought to bring my hiking poles from the plane.

"Help me, Lord. Please help me to stay focused!"

After pausing for several miserable minutes, I gathered my nerves and trudged ahead. The scenery was awesome but may as well have been in black and white. The stress of my precarious situation forced me to resist all distractions, thus robbing me of the ability to absorb the beauty around me. If I allowed my mind to wander, even for a second, it could mean a long, agonizing slide to my demise.

"Death is the penalty for daydreaming," I reminded myself.

It did nothing for my nerves when, quite suddenly, I was surrounded by glaciers. I could feel the cold breeze, like a natural air conditioner, flowing across my face. Though it helped dry the sweat on my brow, I was still glad to be moving further and further from the ice fields.

Finally, after what seemed several torturous hours, the trail widened, the slope yawned gently ahead of me and I rejoiced.

"Safe again!" I shouted. My celebratory words echoed off the surrounding hills.

Mentally and physically exhausted, I desperately needed a place to camp, but every natural feature around me forbade it. The terrain was steep, there were boulders everywhere, and no firewood could be seen. The only potential this place had was as a perfect wind tunnel if the weather worsened. All I could do was continue moving down.

Eventually I came upon a small creek in a ravine. There were treacherous cliffs on either side, but I figured if I just picked my way down, letting the drainage guide me, I'd soon be in more favorable surroundings. My leg, abdomen, and face were pounding with pain.

I must find a place suited for my convalescence. It must be a flat place near the water and protected from the wind. There must be plenty of firewood.

For quite some time, I had been negotiating the terrain along the creek when something to my right grabbed my attention. Smoke.

"Smoke?" I said skeptically.

Curiously, I approached. It wasn't smoke; it smelled like someone was boiling eggs. In an instant, I realized what it was. I smelled sulfur. SULFUR? STEAM? That could mean only one thing:

"HOT SPRINGS!"[5]

Excitedly, I hobbled over to the place. Sure enough, smack dab in the tundra, less than two hundred feet from the creek, was a steaming, luxurious-looking, natural hot springs!

At first, I couldn't accept it as being *real*. What were the chances? Surely, this was a mirage, a dream or simply the consequences of taking too many pills. For a long time I just stood there and stared in disbelief, expecting it to dissipate, to melt away. But thankfully it remained…and so did I.

The entire circumference of the pool was probably eighty to ninety feet. It was lined with skillfully placed stones. It was obvious that something ancient yet refined had been built here. This had been a special place to someone many years ago. I felt as though I was standing on sacred ground.

I finally processed what lay before me and made a crucial decision: if this natural oasis was truly providential (and I believed it was) and not a figment of my imagination (and I believed it wasn't), then I would fully embrace the opportunity and make it my wilderness hospital.

Once this decision had been made, it was easy to throw the load off my back and prepare for my first "treatment." Not until I was completely undressed with my foot in the 100 plus degree bath was I convinced it was "the real McCoy." Oh, man, was it *real*! This was no mirage! Immediately, my flesh and bones and muscles began to absorb the warmth. My entire being, spirit, soul and body, thanked

---

[5] There are estimated to be over one hundred natural hot springs located throughout Alaska. This one is on the USGS map provided at the book's website: www.godofthebrooks.com.

me in unison.

As I soaked up the natural heat, minerals, and sulfur of the pool, I began to notice other more subtle features nearby. There were what appeared to be very old fire pits lined with moss-covered rocks. Several large pockmarks in the earth were all that remained of ancient shelter sites. It soon became obvious that a people, long ago, had taken the time to craft a beautiful place of retreat here. I felt privileged to be partaking of something so hidden, so rare, and, very likely, forgotten.

I thought of my friend whose body was yet on the mountain. He would've loved this place. We had enjoyed many discoveries together over the past twenty-five years. We had stumbled across grayling fossils on the Colville and Chandler Rivers. We had found a hundred year old gold-miner's cabin with everything still intact, as though the prospector had just walked away, expecting to return, but never did. Probably our greatest find, however, was two sets of large bleached moose antlers interlocked, with skulls intact. Obviously, the massive beasts had become inextricably intertwined during battle and either starved to death or became dinner for a pack of wolves.

"Well, Les," I said aloud, "I may have rediscovered an ancient spa but you . . . well, you are discovering the 'Ancient of Days,' the very one who created all of this."

For some time, I thought upon my friend, now gone, and meditated on the descriptions of heaven given in the Bible and on what my buddy might be doing up there this very moment. I took inventory of my own life, impressed with the reality of death. It was a very contemplative, spiritual time. So, while the natural spring healed my body, raw truth healed my soul.

I camped there three days and three nights, soaking, singing, and meditating. I almost cried when, at last, my gear was packed and I was forced by love of life and family to move on. However, the time spent at that miraculous place renewed me in every sense of the word. I named it Paradise Hot Springs.

— 4 —
THE CONTRADICTION

Life is filled with contrasts and contradictions; no sooner had I left Paradise than I encountered the opposite—Hades.

As I followed the creek further down the hill, a large patch of alders impeded my way. Alder bushes are the bane of every mountain man. They are a tangled, hard-to-navigate, obnoxious, cursed, unfriendly, crooked, weed of a tree. They seem to have a distinct personality, and it isn't a nice one. These fought me every inch of the way. Some could be navigated simply by bending over while others forced me to crawl on my hands and knees. This slowed my progress considerably.

I tried to step around a nasty alder on the creek side. Its limbs refused to give way, thus shoving me down with a force so great that it felt as though the thing had literally pushed me in the back. I fell flat on my face in the ice cold water. Fortunately, no bones were broken in the wrestling match, and the only thing bruised was my pride. However, compared to the treacherous spine of Death Mountain, these alders were not so bad. At least I had something to cling to if I did slip while descending the steep hillside.

"I suppose every cloud has a silver lining if you look hard enough," I muttered in disgust.

It took longer than expected, but finally I emerged from the dense vegetation and found myself welcomed by a sentinel of spruce and birch trees. Their branches, still adorned with a few golden leaves, looked like open arms. They were a comforting sight to behold. Even though my aches and pains had revived, I was downright giddy. Here, I felt secure. These soldiers of the Arctic would provide a natural windbreak, abundant firewood, and in places, plenty of leaves that would make for a very comfortable bed. I was elated!

Still high on adrenaline and happy to be in familiar terrain, I hobbled and hurried around like a three-legged chipmunk. Within a couple of hours, I had cut and trimmed a diamond-willow walking stick, built a tarp shelter, chopped wood, started a campfire, and began warming an MRE.

However, my celebration soon came to an end. Intense pain, fatigue, and emotional weakness came upon me. By dark, I was in pitiful shape. I should've been overjoyed. Instead, I moaned myself into a fitful, pain-filled sleep.

The night was long. I dreamt of falling, running from wolves, and even drowning. Several times I awoke, screaming. It must've been a kind of stress release from all that had happened over the past ten or twelve days. In addition, I'm sure the pain meds, though spent, had taken their toll on my mind. I was never so glad to see the sunrise.

After drinking a mug of coffee and consuming half of an MRE, I leaned back against a spruce tree and contemplated my situation. My joy over escaping the crash site was greatly tempered by the pain and fatigue that wracked my body. Every muscle and bone hurt. Time and again, I questioned the wisdom of leaving Paradise Springs. At least while there, my condition had been improving. Now, I felt as though I had been set back. Regardless, I greatly desired to keep traveling. I had gleaned as much as possible from the oasis and must endure the rigors of the journey if I were ever to see my loved ones again.

However, my current condition prevented me from doing so. I was forced by the leg injury to "hole up" for a while longer. I decided then that sunshine, fresh air, spruce needles, berries, boiling water, and one last clean t-shirt with which to make bandages were about all I had for my impromptu wilderness hospital.

The hot springs had done wonders, but I still had a ways to go to realize full recovery.

At least my wound was almost closed now, and the inflammation around it was slowly dissipating but the slightest strain revived the pain.

So, I made some vitamin-packed hot tea using spruce needles, high bush cranberries, rosehips and what few wrinkled blueberries could be found. This concoction also provided a natural antiseptic that was beneficial to me topically as I applied a clean bandage that had been soaked in the hot liquid.

After treating my injuries as best I could, I determined to enact an R&R plan.

I had enough snack food in my pack to last a few days, one more MRE, and plenty of firewood. There was a small seasonal creek nearby, probably fed by the recent snow. The chance of contracting Giardia from this temporary flow was negligible since beavers were the carriers of the parasite and they lived in more permanent waters. The surrounding trees provided protection from the wind. An added blessing was the late season berries that, though not abundant, could still be found. So I decided, based upon these factors that I'd make yet another convalescence camp and, with God's help, heal up completely before moving on.

The next two days were clear, warm, and very therapeutic. My improvement was measurable but slow. I was still weak but gaining ground. The farthest I ventured from camp was about one hundred yards. I feasted on berries, hot tea, and the remaining snacks, which consisted of beef sticks and cheese crackers. Soon those were gone, as was the last MRE.

Hunger got my brain cells swarming. I continued harvesting the berries, using them for both food and drink. I also found and harvested a starchy root that many native tribes use in some of their meals. In Alaska, it's about the diameter of a pencil and tastes like a potato.

The Ahtna tribe in the Copper River valley calls it "Tsaas Root." Other names given to the plant are "potato sausage" and "Indian potato." The Old Ones fried it in moose or bear fat. Some natives still do so today.

I enjoyed a limitless supply of these ingredients for several more days and was lucky enough to snare a snowshoe hare on my third attempt. After skinning and cleaning it, I formulated a frugal, survival recipe:

Place four to six ounces of meat and/or organs in tin mug. Add salt, pepper, and hot sauce (left over from my MREs) and some diced potato sausage root. Boil for twenty minutes and enjoy. This I did each morning and evening.

The hare, once dressed, weighed about 2.5 pounds, including the head. So the little creature along with the Indian potato provided about four days of meager fare.

In addition, I slept in sinfully late and took naps every time I felt tired. Other than gathering firewood, boiling water, and resetting my snares, I did very little. In other words, I lived the life of a retired old man for a while and enjoyed every minute of it.

My only disappointment came at the end of the week when I drank the last of the MRE coffee. I had been miserly with the black gold because I knew once it was gone, I'd become a cantankerous coot with a headache. As expected, the next morning was a sad one. The coffee was gone, and I loved my coffee. In its place, I got the expected pressure in the head.

In spite of the coffee set back, I was finally able to pronounce my wounds healed and my strength increased. Even though food had been a little scarce and I had lost about fifteen or twenty pounds since this ordeal began, it thus far had not affected my energy level. I had been saying for months that I was going to go on a diet but certainly had no idea it would be one brought on by such drastic circumstances.

In addition to the healing of the leg wound, my digestive system was finally back on track, my nose no longer felt swollen, and my eyes, at least when I saw my face reflected in still water, looked normal. So, for all practical purposes, I was a recovered plane-crash survivor. If I could figure out the food dilemma before it killed me, I'd be well on my way to freedom.

I knew I had been very blessed so far. This weather was a rarity for late September in the Arctic. Any day, any hour, conditions could and would change. Freeze-up was just days, maybe hours away. The hiatus I had been experiencing was extremely nice but could end, literally, any minute.

Lately, according to the small thermometer attached to my daypack, the daytime temps had reached as high as fifty degrees Fahrenheit. Nighttime temps were in the teens with heavy frost. I knew from past experience that when snow finally came in Alaska, it came with a vengeance. Old man winter had a bad temper, and he pitched a fit whenever he was late. I needed food and a more protective shelter ASAP.

Sure enough, during the night, heavy clouds blew in. My tarp shelter thundered all night and was a wreck by morning. Snow was imminent.

At first light, I packed up and headed downstream. Very shortly, I was surprised when the creek led me to a major drainage. Had it not been for the wind last night, I would've heard the current hurrying over and around the giant boulders. It was quite a substantial river.

I stood at the confluence and looked both ways like a pedestrian trying to cross a busy street. I really needed to concentrate on where I was and where I needed to go. I was confident that I was on the south side of the Brooks because here trees were abundant. On the north side, trees are practically nonexistent: Spruce, Birch, Aspen and Cottonwood are simply nowhere found north of the Brooks. Most of the foliage on the Arctic slope is made up of blueberry bushes and willows. To my knowledge, there is only one exception.

Years ago Les and I were flying north of the Brooks headed for the village of Umiat. The land below was flat as far as we could see, so we were cruising along at about one thousand feet. Suddenly, into view came what looked like a garden. It was a three to five acre round patch of tall golden-leafed trees. I could not tell whether they were birch or aspen, but to see timber like that so suddenly appear in the midst of hundreds of miles of barren land was stunning. We concluded that someone had planted them there years earlier. Other than this isolated anomaly, I have never seen anything but willow and blueberry bushes north of the big Mountains.

So to go upstream from here would simply lead me right back into the Brooks Range. This I did not want. If I traveled downstream, I'd be headed south.

"Sounds good to me," I said, and turned to the right. I was confident that if I could put enough miles between me and the mountains, I could then turn left or, east, and travel across fairly flat terrain all the way to the Dalton Highway, commonly called "The Haul Road."

The Haul Road begins about eighty miles north of Fairbanks and runs north all the way to Prudhoe Bay, a distance of 420 miles. The road is traveled heavily by big rigs, pipeline security vehicles, service vehicles, tourists, and hunters.

Keeping the towering peaks to my back, I walked along the edge of the large drainage where tundra, spruce trees, and willows gave way to gravel. This is where many animals, large and small, hunt for food, so I decided to do the same. The game trail was quite pronounced. Moose and bear tracks were numerous. Occasionally I crossed wolf scat and beaver tracks. Each time I came upon edible berries, I picked the bush clean. The hunger pangs were increasing every hour.

Maybe I would encounter some game and enjoy a big meal tonight. Better yet, maybe I would see a group of hunters floating by or stumble upon a village. Maybe a plane would fly over and I could light a signal fire quickly enough to be spotted. There were a lot of "maybe's" swirling around in my mind, but one thing was for sure: apart from being found and rescued soon, I must find food. Once I had sustenance, I could then come up with a plan for surviving and, ultimately, escaping this wilderness.

I determined to "hope for the best but prepare for the worst." But what would be "the best"? The best would be to come upon other humans *today* and get flown out of here. Though that was unlikely in such a vast and remote land, my ears, nose, and eyes were constantly tuned in to my surroundings.

And what would be "the worst"? The worst would be to have to walk all the way to the Haul Road. Since we had flown northwest for almost an hour out of Cold Foot at a speed of around 150 knots per hour, I knew I was at least 110 miles from civilization. That distance does not include the zigzag pattern I would be forced into by the nuances of the terrain.

Many challenges lay before me. While walking and grazing on berries, I began to mentally calculate them:

First, there was tundra. Tundra is a moss-covered, spongy bog that sinks anywhere from six to eighteen inches when a person steps on it.

Second, there are tussocks. Tussocks are large mushroom-shaped clumps of grass that are interspersed throughout the tundra. There is barely enough room to walk between the tussocks, and to walk on top of them is almost impossible. They are unstable. It would be very easy to twist an ankle when attempting to traverse them. Negotiating the tundra and tussocks combined strains every muscle from the neck down to the feet. It is a real workout even for someone in perfect health. Sometimes, these hindrances can be circumvented, but oftentimes they cannot.

The third obstacle was the countless rivers that would rise up against me. Some would be narrow and shallow; others, just the opposite, like the one that was beside me. How many awaited me? I did not know, but in spring, summer, and fall they all were so cold as to be deadly.

Fourth, winter weather was overdue in the Arctic. Snow, wind, and freezing temps would threaten me beyond measure. The icy air combined with hurricane-force winds could cause hypothermia and kill me in minutes.

Fifth, I needed more substantial food. Berries and roots alone could not sustain me. I needed protein.

Lastly, a myriad of unpredictable circumstances, such as predators, additional injuries, decreased mental aptitude, and a vulnerable emotional state would fight me all the way.

But for the hand of God, I was alone. It would be me versus the unforgiving Alaskan wilderness. I could not and did not expect any human help. No one had any idea where I was, and Alaska is bigger than almost any three states combined. If I thought anyone back home had even a clue as to our hunting destination or had the ELT not been destroyed in the crash, I would've remained at the base of the mountain, waiting to be rescued.

I thought through all these factors while subconsciously following the game trail. I felt overwhelmed by the vastness of my surroundings. The jagged peaks, the open sky, the loud river, the giant valleys, and the intimidating elements—all seemed to dispute my way. They gathered around me. I felt infinitely small. I was surrounded by the threat of reality, and I was afraid. Discouragement descended upon me. Defeat felt near, almost personified.

Then the snow came. At first, tiny scattered flakes began to fall. Had I been closer to civilization or in a warm house, it would have been a picture-perfect winter scene. Not here. Not today. Within minutes, the cute flurries turned into giant flakes. The wind began howling like a thousand wolves.

Desperately, I needed to find or make a shelter before the storm created "white-out" conditions, when the ground and sky both become solid white. Were that to happen, I would be unable to distinguish the sky from the ground and would lose all sense of direction. The trail was quickly disappearing. Visibility was diminishing every minute.

Straining to discern my way, I barely detected the outline of a large fallen spruce tree about twenty yards to my right. I threw my pack underneath the big, arching branches. Then, dreading the infamous arctic storm, crawled in.

All I could do was hunker down and wait out this temper tantrum of the north. I inserted myself into the sleeping bag first and then wrapped the blue tarp around me. Once I got settled in, my fear subsided.

The "hurricane" that just about blew me off a 3,500-foot cliff a few days earlier must've made a veteran out of me. I had earned a bronze star in that category. For now, just one question concerned me: how long would I have to stay curled up in this uncomfortable position?

— 5 —
THE CAVE

Thankfully, the squall lasted only a few hours. Then, to my delight, the sun emerged. The unpredictability of the weather here was startling. In one day, I had experienced freezing rain, snow, a violent blizzard and now, sunshine accompanied by a magnificent double rainbow! My mind and heart felt like they were tied to a giant pendulum swinging from one extreme to the other.

While packing up, I contemplated how life is much the same. Things can change dramatically in a moment of time. One minute we're strong; the next minute, we're weak. One day we are healthy; the next, sick. One second we're happy; the next second, the phone rings and its bad news. Our lives are in a constant state of change.

The unpredictability of the weather and this journey reminded me of this fact and magnified just how finite I really am. Being made aware of my smallness and God's greatness was good for me. It humbled me. And humility cleanses the soul. About the time I start thinking the world revolves around me, God stops my world. Gently, He reminds me to "be still and know that I am God."

As the sun shone through the trees and the snow began to melt, I felt refreshed in every way. The storm had forced me to stop, to rest, to meditate and to pray, which was just what I needed. The great fear and pessimism that had come over me earlier was gone.

Happy to be on the trail once again, I figured I had about two hours before I'd need to set up camp for the night. I continued to follow the river downstream. It was a big one and getting bigger each moment from the melting snow. The fast-moving main channel had risen dramatically. It was at once impressive and fearsome. Though I expected some river crossings in calculating the journey home, this was my first real gut check. I was intimidated, to say the least. I could not picture myself attempting to cross such a drainage even once, much less multiple times.

As the sky displayed her sunset colors, I pressed on, deep in thought. Maybe in a day or two the water level would drop. Even so, how many more tributaries would I have to cross between here and civilization? At what point would the risk outweigh the gain? The freezing temperature of the rivers could kill me, not to mention the possibility of drowning. Having been raised in Alaska, I was a lousy swimmer. Dog paddling in an ice-cold lake or pond isn't exactly the safest activity. In addition, I certainly did not have the physical strength to swim across this or any other river. Even the narrow, braided headwaters I had seen yesterday flowed strong and fast and were at least, knee deep.

While pondering the challenges that lay ahead, I surveyed the area. I needed to prepare a camp for the night as well as a place to formulate my plan of escape.

Suddenly, I stopped. Through the timber, about a hundred yards to my right, I noticed what appeared to be a well-defined opening at the base of a small hill. It looked like a natural cave. Cautiously, but with great curiosity, I moved toward it. As I drew closer, I realized it was a cave, but it wasn't natural in the least. It was a man-made dugout. My jaw hit the forest floor!

A very old, dry-rotted canvas hung in tatters across the right side of the opening. In spite of the fact that there were no boot tracks in the melting snow, I called out: "HELLO!" No response. Warily, I approached the mouth of the cave.

Using my flashlight, I carefully surveyed the inside. I was stunned. Someone, long ago, had obviously used a shovel to carve this shelter into the side of a small hill. Narrow at the entrance, it widened inside to about eight or ten feet and was seven or eight feet from front to back. I stooped and entered. The ceiling was no more than five feet high.

My light revealed something against the back wall. It was a very crude bed hewn out of a big, peeled, spruce log. Immediately to my right I was startled to see a homemade barrel woodstove. The stovepipe ran up through the dirt and out the top of the shelter. I opened the steel door and shined my light inside. The trough of the barrel had rusted completely through, most likely from years of rainwater running down the chimney into the drum.

The entire scene caused my imagination to go into overdrive. Who would live in these conditions? For what purpose and for how long did someone survive here? I soon spotted my biggest clue. Near the crude bed was a broken pickaxe. Like an archeologist turned detective, I began to piece together a theory: Long ago, someone spent time here prospecting for gold. He was very likely alone and spent at least one winter in this primitive shelter. The pickaxe was probably as much a weapon as it was a tool.

As I searched the outside area, I found a broken shovel, some rusty cans, and—there it was—an old rusty gold pan, half-buried under the moss. Wow! Now my mind really began racing. Was there a stash of gold hidden somewhere? The chances were very slim since most of the men who caught gold fever never made the "big score" or struck it rich.

Restraining my boyish imagination, I focused on more important things. There were a number of items here that could help me survive. At the very least, this would make a great place to rest for the night. As I searched the cave more closely, however, I noticed a clump of dark brown matted hair on the dirt floor. Too coarse to be human hair, it was, no doubt, from a grizzly. This discovery dampened my enthusiasm, to put it mildly. My only comfort was that bears typically don't den up until October, and this was September, albeit *late* September. In addition, the snowfall had been so minimal that I suspected the bears, notorious opportunists, would continue searching for and eating food until the very last minute before hard winter set in. Somehow those thoughts did not comfort me like I thought they should.

By the time I finished gnawing on the subject, I had searched through my gear and made sure the stainless steel hand cannon was fully loaded.

"Yep, 'ole Betsy's got five big 440-grain bullets in her. If you feel like lead for dinner, Mister Griz, you just c'mon and getch ya some," I said, trying my best to sound like a courageous cowboy.

It didn't work. I was as nervous as I was cold. The two combined had me shivering.

Before dark, I gathered boughs from nearby spruce trees and piled them on the rough-hewn bed. I then folded the tarp and placed it on top. This made a crude mattress on the otherwise very hard surface. I unrolled my sleeping bag, made a pillow out of my hunting jacket, and anticipated a good night's sleep. This cave was a real unexpected blessing, or so I thought. Had I known what was about to take place, I would have packed up my belongings and beat a hasty retreat back to Death Mountain.

Reclining on the old miner's bed, I was forced to face reality once again. The miles of tundra, the cursed tussocks, the ice-cold rivers, and the lack of food all combined to make a fast and easy escape impossible. The return home may not happen as quickly as expected.

It was at that moment the thought hit me—hit me so hard I blurted it out loud:

"I might have to spend months here like the old prospector did a hundred years ago!"

Staying here may be the only way to escape the Brooks alive. If I could wait until midwinter, the tundra and the rivers would be frozen. To be sure, travel would be challenging through the snow but would at least be possible. I suppose if the snow got too deep, I could make snowshoes. At least after freeze-up the tundra would be firm and the rivers frozen and thereby crossable. While waiting for winter to do her thing, I could gather, preserve, and build up a food supply for the long journey.

For about an hour I turned each possibility over in my mind, weighing the pros and cons. However risky, a midwinter escape was the only way I could imagine crossing multiple drainages and countless miles of spongy tundra.

Tired as I was, I was too excited to sleep. I went outside, started a fire, and evaluated my options over a cup of rosehip tea: Which scenario presented the greatest risks? Should I attempt the impossible now or wait until midwinter? Which escape plan gave me the greatest advantage? If I waited for freeze up, how could I survive the extreme cold, possibly as low as sixty degrees below zero?

I'd have to figure a way to repair what remained of the rusted woodstove to have any chance of survival. Even then, would I have the patience to wait for at least three months? What about food? Could I trap, fish, hunt, and gather enough to sustain me for at least twelve long weeks?

Thankfully, I had my firearm. It was imperative that I bag a moose, a caribou, or a bear. Only an animal of substantial size could provide me with enough protein to last three months as well as supply the food I would need to make the journey to the highway.

I must make the wisest decision. My life depended upon it. It was no longer about what I *wanted* to do but what I absolutely *needed* to do to survive and get back home.

While the flames turned to embers, I thought of my family and the emotional agony they would soon endure. I had been gone for about three weeks. Ten days was the longest I'd ever spent on a hunting adventure. By now, they would be very concerned. But my decision to go now or wait must not be made based on my emotions or anyone else's. It must be made based on reality. Above all, I wanted to get home *alive*. If that meant slowing down, waiting, surviving, until just the right time then that's what I should do. The more I thought about it and weighed the questions, the answers, the facts, and the fears, the more firmly my mind was set:

"I'm staying till the rivers freeze. Once that happens, I will, with God's help, make the journey to the road. I will begin, at first light, to prepare for winter."

My biggest concern, and therefore my prayer, was for food. Starvation was a real possibility. Nothing else mattered if I did not have groceries. I stood there that night concerned about two things:

Where could I find food? And where was the owner of the long, coarse hair?

— 6 —
THE CHARGE

As the campfire whispered its farewell, I knelt down under the stars and prayed aloud:

"Lord, I'll gather berries and anything else You provide, but please give me meat. I'm going to need protein if I'm going to survive long enough for the rivers and the tundra to freeze. Help me, Lord. Please continue to watch over me. Please protect me from the harsh elements, from wild beasts, and from my own impatience and ignorance. In Your great name, Amen."

Little did I realize how soon and how dramatically God was about to answer my prayer.

By the time I finished petitioning the Lord, the moonlight found its way through the darkness and lay across the shoulders of a weary, hungry man.

I crawled into the crude but warm bed and fell asleep quoting Psalm 27:1:

"The Lord is my light and my salvation; whom shall I fear? The Lord is the strength of my life; of whom shall I be afraid?"

I was "dead to the world," as my mama would say, when suddenly a guttural roar stabbed my brain like a butcher's knife. It sounded like an angry Black Angus bull. I sat straight up in the blackness of night, eyes wide open, straining to see, to know.

"What ? . . who . . . ?" My heart was pounding in my throat.

For a minute, I thought I'd had a nightmare. However, I no sooner came out of the fog of deep sleep than I heard the bellowing noise again and knew exactly what it was. This was no hot tempered bull on a cattle ranch. It was a bear.

He was roaring like a lion and blowing like a wild boar. I'd heard it many times before on numerous adventures.

Then I heard grunting, thrashing, and wheezing. Suddenly, trees started snapping, gravel crunching, and water splashing.

It took only a short while to realize the bear was in a heated battle with another large animal, possibly another bear. It was not unlikely that two bears would be fighting.

I recalled right then how a friend of mine along with his son had been flown in to the Coleville River to hunt caribou. They were successful, but being Cheechakoes, they had piled the meat on a tarp right next to their tent. Sure enough, in the middle of the night, they were awakened by two grizzlies fighting over their caribou meat just feet from where they lay. At one point the animals, insane with rage, literally rolled on top of the tent!

Miraculously, they survived the horrific experience and were the wiser for it. Actually, to the best of my knowledge, they never went hunting again.

But what I was hearing now didn't sound like two bears. Something was different about it. Not until I heard what sounded like a sheet of plywood scraping the willows did I figure it out. A bull moose and a bear were fighting to the death!

I was paralyzed with fear. No doubt the griz was the landlord of the dugout in which I unhappily found myself…and just my luck— it must be a very large bear. An average size six-foot interior grizzly would not normally tackle a mature bull moose. An adult bull moose can weigh up to 1,600 pounds. Judging by the hollow tone the antlers produced every time they hit the brush, this one must be a giant.

"KAWHAP!" "CRAAASH!"

I heard the giants splashing near the river which was at least a hundred yards away yet, in the cold night air, it sounded as if they were just outside the cave.

What if the griz got my scent? This was his den. It had to be his hair I had discovered on the dirt floor. All of these thoughts pierced my mind as the war raged. My pistol was already close at hand, but very quickly, it was *in* my hand.

POP! Another tree broke. "ARRRRUMPH!" The bull grunted. I could hear both animals straining, pushing, stomping. Gravel and rocks clattered like a frightened herd of caribou. Then there was more violent splashing as the river was again disrupted. This pattern repeated itself time and time again, for hours.

I was paralyzed with fear. Then I heard the grizzly's "UHRRHOR-RR!" The barbaric, guttural sound echoed through the entire valley. Surely, every animal within two miles must be in a panic, running away from the bloody contest.

Yet, here I was, scared beyond reason, hoping this was a very bad dream. But I knew it wasn't. Once again, it seemed as though death's icy breath was on the back of my neck. It was then that I heard a blood-curdling noise I had heard only once before in all of my years of hunting Alaska: it was a freakish, primal scream. I knew exactly what it was.

Several years previous, my hunting buddy had dropped a magnificent bull moose on the edge of the forest with his .338 Winchester. Suddenly, a smaller bull emerged looking frightened and confused. Instead of running *from* us, he ran right *at* us! (Bull Moose are quite unpredictable during the mating season.) However, when we stood our ground, he skidded to a halt. As soon as we lifted our rifles, he let out the strangest sound I've ever heard from an animal. It was an angry yet fearful scream. At the time, I could not mentally process what I had just heard—a moose *screamed*!

I think somehow the young bull sensed death, both his comrade's as well as his own, because right then we let him have it from a .375 H&H, and he fell without flinching. I've never forgotten the eerie noise that emanated from that moose's throat, and here I was, listening to it again: a moose's death scream!

"EEEEAAWWW!" The shriek pierced the darkness and rattled my already tormented nerves. It was a skin-crawling experience the first time I heard it and was even more so this time. The beasts continued to fight, but I could tell both were tiring. There were long pauses during which I could hear them gasping like heavyweight boxers in the final round.

I absolutely had to lie down but could not sleep.

Eyes wide open, I held the loaded cannon by my side. Suddenly, right at daybreak, there was a rush, the sound of gravel scattering, willows breaking, a series of muffled growls—and then complete silence. No more roars. No more hooves scraping the rocks. No gasping or heaving. Not a sound could be heard in the gray light of day. My great but hopeless hope was that the giants had killed each other, then I, the man, would be the victor and to the victor goes the spoil.

"Fat chance," I whispered sarcastically.

As I waited for the sun to rise, my body and brain begged for sleep. Finally, under protest but too tired to resist, I lost consciousness. How long I slept I do not know, but when I awoke, sunlight, like a welcome mat, lay brightly on the dirt floor. Quickly and quietly I dressed, strapped the holster across my chest, and slid the .454 inside. Hunched over, I exited the cave, stood very still, and listened.

"Oh how I need coffee," I whispered to myself…"coffee might very well save your life this morning." If ever my brain needed to be wide awake, it was *now*. But the heavenly nectar was not to be had.

It was so quiet I could hear the last of the birch leaves as they landed softly on the frozen ground. The gentle breeze brought the sound of the river to my ears. Then I heard the ravens. Lots of ravens. They must be on the kill.

Were the moose *and* bear dead? Could I be so fortunate?

"I consider myself an optimist but that's going overboard," I said, once again rebuking false hopes.

"More than likely, that big, hairy dinosaur is laid up in those willows, licking his wounds."

Oftentimes, a bear will kill something and bury it just before denning up so that he has a big meal waiting for him when he awakens. No doubt he had claimed this cave as his winter home years ago and the moose was going be his breakfast next spring. He had probably performed this routine for years.

This was his domain, his territory. He wore the badge. His claws were law. And if the hairy sheriff discovered me, I would be considered a trespasser for which the sentence in his jurisdiction, was death.

So, the choice for me was clear: I must either kill this bear or be killed by him. I could wait for the great beast to attack me in the dark, which would be tantamount to suicide, or I could take the fight to him at a time and place of my choosing. I felt like a gunslinger from the old west being forced into a shootout. But the last thing I needed or wanted to do was challenge an Arctic grizzly.

Grizzlies do not have the benefits of salmon-filled streams and moderate weather as their cousin, the Kodiak brown bear does and are thereby smaller. Yet, they have a shorter temper and are more aggressive.

Occasionally, a giant grizzly emerges, seemingly out of nowhere. But, giant or not, aggressive or not, short-tempered maniac or mild-mannered Yogi with a picnic basket, this was life or death for me. I desperately needed that moose meat. And I absolutely did not plan to share the protein or the cave with any wild beast that smelled like rotten carrion.

"Well, Mister Griz," I said in my best Clint Eastwood voice, "here I come."

Once again, I hoped speaking *tough* words in a *tough* tone would somehow produce courage. As before, I was greatly disappointed. Talking tough did nothing for my backbone. But desperation infused me with desire—the desire to live. And to live, I may have to risk dying.

With great caution and my nerves on edge, I proceeded down the trail, limping slightly. Was the stiffness in my knee from my injury, or was I finally feeling old?

"Don't worry about it," I scolded myself, "concentrate!"

As I moved warily down the game trail, closer to the river, all my senses were on high alert.

My right eye lid kept twitching.

The breeze, warmed by the morning sun, was rose gently and brought to my nostrils the smell of blood…and the bear.

The squawking of the ravens became louder. Obviously, they were having a party. I could see them now. Some were watching from the trees in which they were perched, others were gathered in some willows near the river's edge.

The big black birds provided the exact location of the kill for me.

"Where art thou, oh mine enemy?" I whispered, nervously.

My weapon was firmly in my trembling hand as I crept forward, carefully avoiding any dry leaves or twigs.

Where was the bear? Had he been wounded during the fierce battle?

Moose use their front and rear hooves when defending themselves. The force with which they bring these natural weapons down upon their opponents is deadly. They can break a bear's ribs or spine or even crush his skull. For this reason, bears usually avoid fighting with a mature, healthy bull moose unless desperately hungry or…dauntingly huge.

Wolves, on the other hand, are far more likely to attack a full-grown moose because they surround their prey, wear them down, hamstring them, and wait. Once the moose gives up, too tired to fight, the wolves begin feeding on him while he's still alive. They strongly prefer cows with unborn calves. This fact of nature is gory, unpopular, and controversial but nonetheless, true.

For this bear to do battle with a mature bull moose meant one of two things: either the moose, angry and aggressive in the rut, challenged the bear or the bear is very big and preparing his springtime meals in advance. I knew the latter of the two was the more likely scenario.

I moved closer. I was desperate and . . . well, stupid.

Suddenly, I glimpsed a portion of the moose antlers and then the carcass. It was just on the edge of the forest in a large patch of willows about sixty yards away. The bull was dead. His neck was twisted unnaturally, apparently broken. There were huge claw marks on one of his shoulders. The blood had already turned dark.

I waited. My heart was pounding; my skin was tingling. Just as I decided to move forward, the wind began to swirl and touched the back of my neck.

"Oh baby, if the sheriff's in town and catches my scent, that'll do it," I mumbled.

And before I finished reading my fortune cookie—

"POP!" A tree limb snapped, the willows began to sway, and here came one angry, beautifully large beast!

He had bedded down about twenty yards beyond the kill site. As soon as he winded me, he ran straight for his freshly killed prey, woofing and popping his teeth, full of jealous rage.

Until now, I had never witnessed such a display of unbridled anger by such a magnificent creature.

He was huge. He was dark chocolate in color, almost black. He stood half way up and waved his nose in the air, trying to locate the trespasser. Frustrated, he began pouncing on the moose carcass with his front feet. With great vigor, he shook his head, and two gallons of slobber flew in every direction. His horrific roars made my flesh crawl. I had seen other bears do this in an effort to bluff their opponent and escape the fight, but I knew this insane creature wasn't bluffing. I had experienced similar displays a couple of times in my hunting career that were almost comical. This dude wasn't play-acting and neither of us were laughing.

I knew he would charge me as soon as he could locate me. Yet something about him nagged at the backside of my brain. Suddenly I realized what it was. Blood was trickling out of his right eye. He also seemed to be favoring his left side. He winced with every enraged motion. The bull had probably kicked him in the side and broken one or more ribs. Then to my pleasant surprise, blood began coming from his nose. It was bright pink. This could mean only one thing. In jumping up and down just now, his broken rib had punctured a lung!

The great beast would soon be dead even without my help. But there was just one problem. He had a ton of adrenaline coursing through his veins. He had the energy to tear me and ten others to shreds before finally expiring. The grizzly and brown bears are famous for the damage they can do and the distance they can run with their heart blown to pieces. This dude's moments were numbered, but I could still be his last meal, so to speak.

These thoughts swirled in my mind and without thinking I lifted the gun. He caught the movement, located me, and charged, full tilt.

"You big dummy!" I scolded myself. "All you had to do was wait and he would've expired." It was too late. There wasn't even time for a short sermon.

I was shocked by the great distance he covered with every leap. I calculated his speed and my location. I had five seconds, max. He came with haste—5, 4, 3, then 2 . . .

It was very difficult to take the extra time to aim, steady my hand, exhale, and pull the trigger. But I must. The first shot had to count. If it didn't, the moose would be his entrée; I'd be his dessert.

"BOOM!" The pistol roared and the bear roared back.

He staggered and bit himself in the chest, the point of impact. Instantly, he regained his composure and kept coming. By the time I recovered from the recoil of the huge gun, he was at point blank range.

"BOOM!" Again, a thumb-sized piece of lead shot from the barrel. I had no clue if that one hit him, because at the same time the gun fired, I took a step back to avoid the beast…and tripped… and fell!

But that clumsy, backwards, wonderful blessing-of-a-fall saved my bacon.

In his rush to destroy me, in his great hurry to kill me, in his wicked rage, the bear leapt so high and jumped so far that when I fell backwards, he completely overshot me. I rolled onto my stomach just in time to see him flip in midair like a one thousand-pound cat. His dexterity was beyond impressive!

Once again, here he came and in a split second he was right above me.

"BOOM!" For the third and final time, the blast of the hand cannon echoed off the mountains. I saw the impact of the 440-grain bullet. It had tremendous velocity, traveling at 2,400 feet per second. It slammed into the great bear. He dropped, kicked his back legs several times, and was stone dead. The third and final chunk of lead had entered at the base of the throat and exited just behind the head. The bullet had taken meat, hide, spine, and his ability to move with it. He flopped like a rag doll, jerked in seizure-like spasms for about 3 seconds and exhaled, loudly. I knew he was dead—real dead.

I was on my stomach so I just lowered my head between my outstretched arms until my forehead touched dirt. My fingers were still glued to the gun. I was too stunned to comprehend what had just happened. The suddenness of the charge, the ringing in my ears, the smell of gunpowder, and the stench of a huge, dead griz was a lot to absorb.

When I finally did try to stand, I began to shake uncontrollably. My legs turned to water, so again I lay down, this time, flat on my back.

After several quiet minutes, I opened my eyes, looked up at the clear, blue sky and said,

"Lord, what have we done?"

Exhausted yet relieved, I momentarily fell into a deep sleep.

— 7 —
THE CARCASSES

My eyes opened when something gently touched my face. It was snow. I couldn't help but lie there and contemplate the irony that a thousand-pound bear put me to sleep and a tiny snowflake woke me up.

"Man, that felt good," I whispered. Slowly, I moved into a sitting position and saw the giant bear, dead, just a few feet away. That cleared my cranium instantly!

He looked like a small mountain. I stood, brushed the dirt off myself and respectfully walked around my deceased enemy. He was at least a nine-foot bear. I would "square" the hide later.[6] For record book purposes, an official measurement of the length and width of the skull was required, but I didn't care about such things, especially at the moment. My primary concern was twofold: I was alive and the bear was dead. In addition, the protein and warmth the two animals could provide me in the coming months would be the difference between starvation and survival. This was a tremendously unexpected blessing and answer to prayer. "And not a moment too soon," I said as the snow began to descend heavily.

Leaving the griz, I determined to skin and butcher the moose first since its meat was far more desirable than griz. Black bear meat is very tasty, similar to pork. But grizzly meat isn't similar to anything. It's just not as good, in my opinion, as black bear or moose. In spite of that, the fat and hide from the big bear would be extremely useful, and I determined not to waste the meat either. However, due to my proclivity towards moose meat, the big bull would receive my immediate attention.

---

[6] Squaring a hide is done by measuring the length from nose to tail, the width from paw to paw, adding those two numbers together and dividing by two. This is how hunters, trappers, and taxidermists determine the size of an animal hide.

As I approached the kill, the ravens scattered and loudly squawked. I'm sure they said some rather unpleasant things about me. It didn't matter. They'd get their share soon enough. Ravens are very intelligent birds and for that reason are revered greatly by Alaskan natives. In the Bible, they were used by God to feed one of the most famous Old Testament prophets, Elijah, and were used by Noah as scouts in the days following the great flood. So I would not begrudge them a portion. But for now, they must watch and wait because God had answered *my* prayer! The significance of that truth was finally settling in: God had answered my prayer.

With great respect and gratitude, I walked around the kill site, smiling so big my face hurt.

"Thank you, Lord. Wow! That was a little dramatic, don't You think? That's not exactly the way I would've chosen to gather protein, but You do work in ways that oftentimes surprise Your children. I give You the praise and thanks and the glory!"

The ground all around the moose was greatly disturbed and looked as though a dozen hand grenades had exploded within a twenty-yard radius. Every willow bush and small tree nearby was mowed down. In spite of the falling snow, blood and mucus was still visible in the churned-up sand. But there, on the edge of the battlefield, lay the giant moose. He probably weighed 1,200 to 1,400 pounds. He had a heavy set of antlers. They were at least sixty inches wide, with five brow tines on one side, four on the other. I could tell by the scars on his rack that he'd been in some nasty brawls with other bulls. No doubt he'd been fighting his comrades over the right to breed cows. He also had a very strong, musky odor, which is typical during the rut, or mating season.

The odor comes from the moose urinating in "wallows," or mud holes, and then rolling around in it. This barbaric cologne really gets the cows' attention. (The odor of rutting moose gets my wife's attention as well when I return from a successful hunt, just not in the same way.)

He had fallen on his side, so I simply began the skinning process. I made an incision behind the head and ran the knife down the spine, all the way to the tail. After making a few other cuts around the neck and down the legs, I hurriedly peeled the hide back and began to remove the back straps.

The straps are located on both sides of the spine and on a full-grown moose are four to five inches thick, four to five inches wide, and three to four feet long. There are two per animal, and together they weigh in excess of thirty pounds. Their location on the moose causes the straps to be very succulent since they do nothing but lie there and tenderize. These and the tenderloins were my two favorite cuts.

I was starving before I even began the butchering process, so the handling of these prime pieces of meat pushed me over the edge. I did not care that it was snowing.

I started a fire and roasted a thick fillet. As the chunk of tender meat accepted the flames from the burning spruce, the juice began to fall onto the orange embers and sizzling could be heard in the forest. "Man has arrived," I stated emphatically.

The odor of roasted steak and wood smoke swirled around my head as did a thousand grand emotions. In addition, the late-season high bush cranberries nearby made an excellent side dish. I ate until I was gloriously gorged.

While savoring every bite of my five-star meal, I again contemplated the violent struggle between these two creatures. The moose could have initiated the conflict just as easily as the bear since Bull Moose are very agitated during the late fall season. Their hot temper often results in their demise. Over the years, we have successfully called in rutting bulls by imitating the challenging calls of an opponent. On one particular hunt, we actually had a moose come right into camp while we were chopping firewood. He thought the sound of the axe hitting the tree was a call to battle. To say that Bull Moose are short-tempered and aggressive this time of year is an understatement.

Obviously, these warriors who lay dead less than a hundred yards from each other had crossed paths while in a foul frame of mind. I'd never know for sure which one had started this battle to the death, but one thing I did know: both ended up in the wrong place at the wrong time, especially when they woke me up from what had been a good sleep.

I thought of a poster hanging in my man cave back home that

reads, "Every morning a caribou wakes up knowing it must outrun the fastest wolf or be killed. Every morning a wolf wakes up knowing it must outrun the slowest caribou or starve to death. Whether you're a wolf or a caribou, when I wake up, you'd better be running." I couldn't help smiling recalling those lines. Of course, I was just enjoying the moment. Deep down inside I knew who the ultimate victor really was: my Creator, Sustainer, and Redeemer, the Lord Jesus Christ. In all honesty these two giants were a huge blessing from God. I'd best not become proud, but was I happy? I was definitely happy!

Returning to the moose, I removed the front and rear quarters. The shoulders on a big moose weigh 75-85 pounds—each. And just one rear quarter can weigh 125 pounds. Currently unable to carry such heavy loads, I simply brought the tarp from the cave to the carcass and rolled the huge pieces of meat directly onto one half of the plastic and then covered it with the other half. I knew if I kept the meat clean, cool, and dry, I'd have many more pleasant dining experiences while camped here and more than enough protein for my journey to the road.

Darkness was near so I hurried. With the shoulder and rear quarter from one side removed, I sliced the meat from between the ribs and placed it in a separate pile. That and the brisket would make good jerky. The gut sack came out next, which made it possible to remove the heart and liver, roll the carcass over, and repeat the process. The neck meat and one shoulder I donated to the ravens because it had been tainted by the bacteria-filled teeth and claws of the bear. By the time I had three of the quarters, the back straps, tenderloin, and rib meat off, I was exhausted. I headed straight for the cave. Full of fire-roasted moose meat and cranberries, I pulled off my boots and have no recollection of anything after that until the ravens woke me up late the next day.

"Caw! Caw! Wauk-uk! Wauk-uk!" they squawked. I interpreted that to mean "Thank you! Thanks a lot! Thanks a lot!" Even though ravens have more voice inflection than most animals, I couldn't tell if they were being sarcastic or not. Oh well, at least I wasn't running for office.

I set upon the moose once again and completed the task in about two hours, including the removal of a large portion of the hide. It would be just as useful as the bear skin. Then I took a late but long lunch break that included a repeat of yesterday's menu, followed by a well-deserved nap. Afterwards, I turned my attention to the great bear.

Already too tired to complete the daunting task of skinning and quartering the bear, I decided to simply get a start on it and complete the job the next day. I could tell I still did not have the stamina or normal strength I had before the crash. I had to embrace the fact that I was still recovering. I knew I must be wise and pace myself. The meat and the hides would not spoil in these cold temperatures. Therefore, I skinned the back half of the bear, covered everything, and quit for the day. It was time to clean up, eat, and get some sleep.

Having not bathed in quite a while, I decided to do so in the river. After locating a calm back eddy that I guessed to be about four feet deep, I did the polar plunge. It was unbelievably painful! The water felt like liquid ice. Immediately, my limbs started cramping. It felt like an ice-cream headache, but the pain wasn't in my head. Instead, it throbbed in my hands and arms and legs.

Instantly, I stumbled out of the freezing water and onto the riverbank. For at least ten minutes, I rolled around on the ground in agony. I began to vigorously rub my flesh to restore circulation. This experience confirmed that my decision to not swim, raft, or wade across these arctic rivers was a good one.

The feeling of putting on dry, warm clothes was at once comforting. And just to generate a little more body heat, I jogged to the respective kill sites and placed rocks on top of both meat piles so that no fox, martin, lynx, or other small creatures could spoil my supply—or so I thought. My biggest concern was that another hungry creature roaming the area might discover my stash and mark it for itself. Many animals have the nasty habit of urinating on what they claim. None of my recipes called for such an ingredient, nor would my taste buds celebrate such an encounter.

With light fading fast, I headed for the dugout and prepared for the night. By now, I was really feeling the pain of success. A comfortable night's sleep was a must. As soon as I reclined, the full impact of the past two days hit me hard and fast. I knew I had really overdone it. The fatigue was so intense that I felt nauseated. My head was throbbing, I was dizzy, and once again my legs began to cramp. I screamed in agony yet was fully aware that these symptoms were not due to the injuries I had sustained in the crash or even the consequences of the polar plunge. These symptoms were indicative of dehydration. Beginning tomorrow, I must drink more water.

Thirsty I may be, but at least I wasn't hungry, and the thanks belonged to God. Less than forty-eight hours earlier, I had prayed and asked the Lord to supply my needs. He had more than answered my prayer. I could not help but thank Him between leg cramps. After about half an hour of intermittent torture sessions, the pain subsided, and I fell into a deep and peaceful sleep.

The day was bright and the sun high by the time I arose. Everything outside was white. About three inches of "termination dust" had fallen. Alaskans refer to the first snow each winter as termination dust because the fall season is considered terminated once everything is covered in white. In the interior, we jokingly say that we have only two seasons: spring and winter. Unfortunately, there are some years when that saying is far too close to the truth.

Even though the white stuff had come and gone twice in the past few days, I suspected winter was officially here and would remain in the arctic for at least seven months.

However, with the beautiful new season came a new problem. The glare of the sun reflecting off the snow was blinding. I began to experience headaches and to see black squiggly lines writhing everywhere I looked. The remedy I chose was an ancient one used by Alaskan natives. I constructed a pair of birch-bark sun shields. The goggles covered my eyes with only a very narrow slit to look through. I tied them around my head with 550 cord and found immediate relief. Snow blindness was not on my wish list this winter. It is a uniquely painful experience and produces excruciating pain behind the eyes, migraine-level headaches, and nausea. It could, if not addressed, damage my vision permanently.

Once my eyes adjusted to the primitive sunglasses, I perused the meat stash and the kill site from a distance. Everything appeared the same as when I left it last evening. I was encouraged. However, after the exertions of yesterday, every muscle was hurting, my left leg was pounding, and my back was as stiff as a gnarly diamond willow. In this condition, it was difficult to imagine having to walk a hundred and fifty-plus miles across the wilderness.

I paced back and forth in front of the cave just to work out the kinks in my body. Next, I built a fire, purified a quart of water, and drank every bit of it, recalling the painful cramp attacks of the previous night. My morning meal consisted of fresh moose liver, cranberries, and several cups of rosehip tea. Once it all started kicking in, I felt limber and re-energized.

"Today, I will finish skinning the bear," I said to myself as I walked down the trail.

Since the moose meat was safe and dry for now, I'd skin the bear and harvest the fat. If I could accomplish those two tasks today, tomorrow I'd take advantage of the quickly disappearing cranberries and rosehips. Soon they'd be gone. I must have something else in my diet besides meat. I prayed the Lord would hold back the winds. Late season berries remain when protected from the windstorms that frequent these mountain areas. Though shriveled and overly ripe this time of year, the rosehips and high bush cranberries can hang on quite a while into the winter months if undisturbed. I would search for more of them tomorrow, but for now, the bear carcass was calling.

From working on the heavy beast the day before, I knew that completely skinning it was going to be challenging and rigor mortis wouldn't make the task any easier. Sure enough, I soon found myself in a wrestling match with a very stiff carcass. In addition, the fact that the animal probably weighed a thousand pounds and hadn't gotten any lighter forced me to gut it. I had hoped to avoid the extra trouble and mess of removing the entrails, but there was no possible way I could roll this bear over without ridding it of some weight.

Because of my fatigue and the greatness of the beast, I eventually had to resign myself to salvaging just the major portion of the hide. Leaving the pelt on the legs and head, I salvaged only the cape from the torso. I just did not have the strength to physically manipulate this creature into a position where I could skin the entire animal.

It did not matter. It was so big, the portion of hide I did remove would provide more than enough material for warmth. There was also an abundance of fat, which would be useful for food and candles. It took me about two hours, but when completed, I had a hide that measured seven feet long and five feet wide. Even with the head and legs missing, the size of the rug was impressive. Soon I would need to flesh the hide and figure out a way to soften and preserve it. Once this was done, it would prove invaluable to my survival.

The layer of fat on the animal was tantalizing. It was at least four inches thick. I hoped it tasted as good as it looked. Black bear fat tastes better than butter. If grizzly fat is even close, I'd have a very rich and tasty item to add to my menu once it was rendered. Rendering is the result of heating the fat until it liquefies and then skimming it. Once the undesirables are removed and the grease cools, a delectable creamy butter remains that is extremely savory. At least that had been my experience with black bear fat. Time would tell whether grizzly fat could measure up to the standard. My hopes were high, and I began to salivate as I recalled a very enjoyable, albeit rugged, dining experience of years gone by.

I was a guest in the Athabaskan village of Huslia. I had been invited to sing and read Scripture to "Grandma Mary" who, at ninety-five years of age, was about to go to heaven. She had a very clear testimony, in word and deed, of knowing Christ as her Lord and Savior.

While there, her grandson shared dried moose jerky and black bear fat with me. I was slightly apprehensive at first, but upon tasting the ancient combination of smoke-dried moose jerky dipped in ice-cold bear butter, I pushed aside my manners with reckless abandon and requested more. My host swelled up with pride, handed me another stick of jerky, and, grinning from ear to ear, the jar of cold bear butter. I could not have hidden my delight had I tried. The combination of protein and fat was both rich and delicious.

Animal fat can also be burned slowly and used much like kerosene for lantern fuel. For thousands of years, the Inupiat Eskimos have used polar bear fat, whale blubber, or seal oil for light and heat. They put the oil from melted fat in a small vessel, place a string or small piece of rope in it, and light one end. The string acts as a wick, drawing the oil out and feeding the little flame at the other end. It burns just like a wax candle.

I would soon be very dependent upon this ancient practice.

If my calculations were correct, it was October 1 or 2. The northland had gradually been losing daylight since June 22. The days were far shorter than they were in the spring and summer. In one more month, I'd have just two to three hours of useable sunlight per day. At high noon, the sun would appear just above the horizon. Without a lantern, candle, or bright moon, I'd be unable to read or venture outside. This could result in a condition known as cabin fever. As a result of long hours of darkness and inactivity, many a prospector or trapper has been driven crazy with cabin fever.

I must prepare now to combat this psychological disease. Since my flashlight batteries would last only another week or two, the animal fat candles would enable me to enjoy some light in the cave and to read my little hunting Bible, thus staving off the dreaded fever. In addition to having light, staying busy for the next ten to twelve weeks would also strengthen my mental condition. To that end, I set some goals:

First, I would smoke and dry enough moose meat to last the duration. The colder it got, the more difficult it would be to do this properly, so time was of the essence.

Second, I'd flesh and tan the animal hides to make them more useful. This also needed to be done before hard cold set in.

Third, I'd build and test a pair of snowshoes.

Lastly, I'd read through the New Testament by candlelight and memorize the book of 1 John, all five chapters.

Working towards these objectives would keep me mentally, physically and spiritually active during the dark season, and that would be good medicine. With these thoughts in mind, I made many round trips to the kill sites and carried meat, fat, and skins to the cave. I put the bounty in three separate piles, just feet from the entrance, and covered them.

The weather was cold enough that preservation was not a concern, but varmints and ravens were. However, if any creature tried to steal from me, I still had two rounds left in my hand cannon, and

I was in no mood to share. "Possession," they say, "is nine-tenths of the law," especially in the wild. But with my pistol, I felt I held ten-tenths. As long as there wasn't an eleventh part unknown to me, I should be fine.

"I already gave at the office!" I announced, regularly and loudly.

Most wild animals are more afraid of the human voice than they are of a gunshot. In addition to yelling frequently and talking to myself out loud, I urinated regularly around my food supply. This was a crude language but one understood by the animal kingdom.

That afternoon, I lay a giant steak on a bed of hot coals and contemplated my to-do list. Fleshing and preserving the hides would be the most daunting task on the list. Fleshing is a process of removing all of the meat, fat and excess tissue from the backside of the pelts. Although I did not have a fleshing board or draw knife, I could improvise by using a smooth log and my hatchet blade.

Unfortunately, I did not have the necessary chemicals to tan the hide. Without putting it through the tanning process, it would stiffen, greatly limiting its usefulness. I had heard from native friends that in the old days human urine and animal brains were used to tan pelts. The acid, it was said, would break down the hide tissue, creating a soft, supple blanket. "That hide would have to be mighty nice to overcome the thought of a urine-soaked blanket," I said wryly. Turning the raw hides into useful material must be done soon, but how? I'd have to figure that one out pronto.

For now, however, I needed food. I was wet from the snow and very tired. I could tell, based on the fading light of early winter, it was already mid-afternoon. The moose steak was soon cooked perfectly: charbroiled on the outside, red and juicy on the inside. It must've weighed a pound and a half, but it disappeared in less than five minutes. I undressed, hung my clothes up to dry, and crawled in for the night.

First thing tomorrow, I thought, I'll pick as many of the late-season berries as possible. These would be invaluable to my survival. The vitamin C would greatly aid in my recovery and would help balance my high-protein diet. The berries would be scattered but still numerous based on what I had seen today. I would need to craft some containers in which to gather and store them . . . Sometime during that thought process, logic was replaced with snoring.

The following day, as soon as I stepped outside the cave, I knew it was going to be a good day. Even though it was windy and noticeably colder, I made my way to the trail below and located a good-sized birch tree. After cutting two large pieces of bark from the tree, I baptized them in the river several times until they were soaked and flexible. I then returned to the cave site, cut slits into each corner and shaped them into rectangular baskets. Using my knife, I punched holes through each fold and cinched the corners together using strips of willow bark.

Finally, I dried them over the fire. As expected, they retained their shape and provided me with two rustic but useful berry baskets capable of holding about a half-gallon each. This process is used by Alaska natives to make baskets and moose calls, though the end result when an Athabaskan grandma makes one is no doubt far superior to mine. Being my first, they were rougher than a child's VBS craft. But they were sufficient.

The high bush cranberries were the last to drop. They would be my primary focus. There were also some shriveled rosehips scattered throughout the woods. Since both grew relatively high off the ground, the snow hadn't yet covered them. It didn't take long to harvest quite a few. I did not try to separate them. Both were good to eat and highly nutritional.

By noon, I had almost filled the containers, so I decided to return to the cave for food and rest and to deposit the berries. An hour later, I returned to the harvest. I had been gathering more fruit for just a few minutes when, suddenly, I saw movement to my right, near the kill sites. I stopped in midstride. There, not fifty yards away was a wolverine! He had already spotted me. With one paw suspended, he glared into my eyes.

— 8 —
THE CARNIVORE

The situation in which I found myself was completely unpredictable. Wolverines are famous for their ferocity and short temper. Yet they are also very shy and elusive. Many woodsmen consider them to be the cagiest of all the animals. They are void of fear and, if stirred to anger, prefer violence over peace any day of the week. Not expecting to encounter any dangerous game, I had left my pistol in the shelter. All I had for my defense was my walking stick. It might as well have been a daisy against this devil.

Clearly, the wolverine had been drawn to the remains of the moose and bear, which by now were mostly scattered bones and some hair. Everything else had been taken by me and the ravens. Wolverines, however, have such powerful jaws that they can crush the bones of large animals and eat the marrow. Obviously, this wily creature had claimed the moose remains and viewed me as an interloper.

Even though I half expected him to attack me, I was nevertheless shocked when he bounded straight toward me! I immediately went into high gear, dropped my walking stick, threw down the basket of berries, and grabbed a tree limb. I was in no shape to climb a tree, but full of adrenaline, I was instantly six feet off the ground, hugging the spruce like a frightened bear cub. The wolverine was soon underneath me, spitting, fuming, and urinating all over my cranberries and rosehips! I spit and fumed right back at him, mimicking the noises he made. The baskets were saturated with urine and completely ruined! I'd have to start all over just because mister-devil-with-a-temper was having a tantrum!

Angrily, he circled the tree, eyes full of hatred. I noticed his tail was missing, and as I looked more closely, I could see that one of his front paws was also gone. In its place was a leathery stump. He also had scars on his face. He tried baring his teeth at me in a show of defiance, but they were so worn down that about all I saw were blackened gums. It would've been humorous had I not been at such a disadvantage. Obviously, this was an old battle-worn creature of the Arctic who had survived traps, fights with other wolverines, attacks by wolves, and probably even some wrestling matches with grizzlies. I could not help admiring the nasty critter. "Get outta here!" I yelled.

For a moment, I felt brave. Then I saw myself from a third-person point of view—desperately clinging to a tree, trembling from an overdose of adrenaline, and yelling at a small animal that, as it turned out, was already nonchalantly walking away. He casually sauntered to the bone yard, picked up a bone, and then sauntered into the forest. I could sense he despised me. "Better to be despised than defeated!" I shouted. "Next time, I'll be ready!"

Once on the ground, I carefully inspected the baskets, hoping at least one of them had escaped the devil-spray.

"No such luck," I grumbled. This was one, mean, old, malicious wolverine. I had no doubt that, with hardly any teeth, he was hungry as well.

Right then I thought of our evil unseen enemy who the Bible says walks about "as a roaring lion seeking whom he may devour" [1 Pet. 5:8]. Yet for those who have embraced "the tree," trusting in the death, burial, and resurrection of the Lord Jesus Christ for the forgiveness of their sins, Satan is powerless. He has no teeth. All he can do is snarl, spit, and fume.

Once the old man of the woods was long gone, I cautiously retreated to my fortress and rested awhile, pistol in hand. My efforts at berry picking, for now, had been stalled, but I was not about to quit. I was determined that this defeat was only temporary and to use it to improve my circumstances.

Over the next few days, I crafted two more baskets, larger than the previous ones, and continued picking. Each time I filled them with fruit, I deposited the bounty inside the cave. Cranberries, rosehips, and a few remaining blueberries made up the harvest.

And I determined never again to venture outside without my handgun.

Thankfully, my strength and stamina were increasing. I guessed that it had been over a month since the crash. My leg wound was barely noticeable. My nose was a little crooked but completely healed. The intermittent pain in my abdomen was no longer an issue, and my digestive system was back to normal. The final healing of my injuries came not a moment too soon.

The list of things that needed to be done to survive this unforgiving wilderness was daunting. At the top of that list was turning the bear and moose hides into something useful. The warmth these potential blankets could provide was indispensable to my surviving the deep freeze that was now upon me. Somehow I must tan them, and to do that, I must remove every bit of flesh and fat from the hides. I dreaded the laborious task of fleshing but knew it must be done. The chore would be even more difficult because of the decreasing temperatures. The temps had dropped by fifteen to twenty degrees just in the last few days. Daytime temperatures were ten to thirty above; nighttime temps were creeping below zero. My sleeping bag did not feel as warm as it had just a week ago. Soon I would need to repair the woodstove and gather firewood. Next on the list, however, was the fleshing of the hides.

It took some searching, but I finally located a smooth spruce log to use as a fleshing board. I then got a good-size campfire going to warm the skins, making them easier to manipulate. With great effort, I unrolled the stiff griz hide, hair side down, draped it over the log, and began scraping the excess fat and tissue with my hatchet. It was tedious, painstaking work. However, knowing the importance of this rug, I pressed on, stopping just long enough to sharpen my hatchet blade on a flat river stone and feed the fire.

The process took the entire day. By sunset, however, I had a *very* clean bearskin. What little flesh and fat I couldn't scrape off with the hatchet, I had tediously removed with my knife. After carefully inspecting every inch of the pelt, I was satisfied that I had in my possession the perfect material for a blanket, parka, poncho, or any number of other things. It still needed tanning, but I believed the most difficult phase to be over. Tomorrow, I would do the same to the moose hide and then try to tan them together using nothing but smoke and a stick. Theoretically, the smoke would cure the hides. The stick would be used to beat them every hour for as long as the process took to keep them pliable. I hoped it worked because the more supple the skins were, the more useful they would be.

I could not help being reminded that God wants me to be the same way: pliable, willing, and surrendered to His Word, the Holy Bible. Otherwise, I am of little use to my Creator. This thought tugged at my soul late into the night. My conscience was disturbed. I had spent much of my time on earth doing life my way instead of God's way. "Lord," I prayed, "give me the faith and strength to follow the path You have carved for me. I don't want my life to be wasted. Help me to glorify Your name in everything I think, say, and do. Please make me more like Your divine Son, the Lord Jesus Christ. May I become more flexible, more pliable, in Your hands for Your kingdom and Your glory." After much consternation and prayer, sleep finally descended upon me. Once it did, I slept soundly, blanketed by the peace of surrender.

It was late into the day by the time I had risen and eaten breakfast. I sat outside on a stump-turned-chair, nursing a cup of hot tea. I yearned for a strong cup of black gold—coffee. "Just one cup each morning sure would be nice," I muttered. But the mug of rosehip and spruce-needle tea I held in my hands wasn't bad for a backup brew. At least it was hot.

While contemplating the approaching day's tasks, the reality of the Arctic winter began to settle upon me. It was mid-October, and the temps continued to drop. During the night, for the first time, it hit ten degrees below zero. That was as low as my little daypack thermometer could register. It seemed as though each day I was forced to wear more clothing. This morning, I had put on a full set of long johns, blue jeans, a quilted shirt, my hunting jacket, a wool hat, wool socks, and my hunting gloves; yet I was still feeling the bite of hard winter. "I must figure out how to repair this rusty old woodstove," I said aloud. "It will not only help me survive the cold but will also provide a place suitable to cure both of the hides."

Years earlier a friend of mine who owned the local fur tannery had shared with me a brief history of the tanning process. He was the one who had told me of the urine and brain recipe, which I had, for obvious reasons, rejected. But I remembered another ancient method he had described. It was the "smoke and strike" method.

Under the circumstances, this was probably the only feasible process available to me, so I focused my attention on turning the cave into a temporary smokehouse.

The homemade stove inside the cave had been built long ago using a thirty-gallon steel drum. It was obvious that over the years rain and snow had entered through the stovepipe and collected at the lowest point in the barrel. The trough or "belly" had, over time, rusted through. How could I patch the disintegrated bottom of the stove? I then remembered the old cans, shovel, and gold pan I had found when I first discovered the dugout. It took a while to locate them under the snow, but soon I had several items, all made of metal, in my hands. The cans themselves were brittle and useless, but the gold pan and shovel were in decent shape. Excited, I felt as though I had uncovered buried treasure, because now I had just what I needed.

Using the pan, I patched the bottom of the barrel by simply cradling it in the trough that had long since rusted through. There was still plenty of support on each side of the pan. This would serve as the new base and hold, at least, some wood. I then went outside and placed the shovel on top of the stovepipe, concave side up. Then I placed a rock inside the concaved side of the shovel. The rock would hold the crude cap in place. Together, the shovel head and rock would prevent the smoke from escaping too quickly and help convert the cave into a smokehouse.

As dilapidated as it was, the stove would help provide smoke for the tanning of the skins and, later, warmth during extreme cold snaps. The entire setup was one notch below primitive, but I didn't care. For now, all I needed was to hang the hides just inside the mouth of the cave and get as much smoke as possible for as long as possible on those hides. With everything ready, I crawled inside the cave, lit the kindling in the stove, fanned the flames, and added some dry spruce that would soon develop into a nice bed of red-hot coals. It took about half an hour, but eventually, I had a blaze-orange foundation. A couple of chunks of cottonwood[7] and some

---

[7] Cottonwood is considered by most sourdoughs to be the lowest-quality firewood in Alaska. It smolders more than it burns. That's why many Alaskan natives use it to "cold smoke" their fish. The

green spruce boughs were all it took, and the smoke factory worked like a charm!

Once the spruce boughs and cottonwood started billowing, I exited the dugout, coughing and sputtering like an old Model T. I then hung both hides just inside and beat them with a stick about every half hour. Several times during the long process I had to endure the smoky cave in order to rekindle the fire and add more spruce boughs and cottonwood. At times, it was quite painful to my eyes, lungs, and brain. This routine continued throughout the day and into the night. Not once did I get cold. I was almost always moving. I was either gathering more wood or beating hides or melting snow for drinking water. I stopped to eat just twice. All day and into the night I worked on those skins.

The process took longer than expected, but finally, just after daybreak, the skins began to feel really supple. I was ecstatic.

It felt really good to accomplish a very important task using such a primitive method. The reward was more than pleasant. It was life. To be sure, the skins were not professionally tanned by any stretch of the imagination, but they were certainly far more useful than they had been in their former condition. The age-old method had worked. The task had not been easy, but the recipe was simple, requiring just fire, cottonwood, and a stick, all three of which I had at my disposal. I now had blanket and clothing material suitable for extremely low temperatures.

However, the project had taken a lot out of me. Some of the old wounds had revived, and extreme fatigue was haunting me once again. In addition, the continual barrage of smoke upon my brain, eyes, and lungs had taken its toll. My ability to think logically was greatly reduced. I started feeling dizzy, off balance.

During the process, I'd been melting and drinking snow water and eating moose jerky. Obviously, it hadn't been nearly enough considering all of the calories I had expended. I needed to rehy-

---

(cont.) cold smoking method requires very little heat. It depends primarily upon smoke and time to cure the fish. The natives have used this method for thousands of years to preserve their catch. It was the smoldering aspect of the cottonwood that was useful to me in this situation. It extended the smoking time, thus minimizing the number of trips I had to make inside the cave as well as the amount of wood needed.

drate and refuel my body *now*. So, for the remainder of the day, I drank what must've been half a gallon of hot rosehip tea, cooked and consumed a giant moose steak, and took a sinfully long nap outside the cave. That night, with the northern lights fluttering overhead, I added fresh spruce boughs to my bed, threw my sleeping bag back inside, and snored the shovel off the stovepipe.

— 9 —
THE CANDLE

Firewood was next on my survival list. I had depleted more than anticipated to cure the hides. Since the crippled stove could not handle the weight of full-sized pieces of birch or spruce, I focused my search on kindling and small- to medium-sized fallen trees, around three to five inches in diameter. The only tool I had for woodcutting was my camp hatchet. It wasn't really a premium quality tool designed for heavy use, so I knew I must treat it with care. If lost or broken, I'd be relegated to breaking branches by jumping on them, and that would increase both my workload and my risk for injury. Therefore, I used the valuable tool methodically and cautiously, taking my time. Nevertheless, after just one full day of concentrated cutting and stacking, my woodpile really began to swell. Fortunately, the area inside the cave was so small that it wouldn't take much heat to make a big difference. The problem would be maintaining the fire for long periods of time so as to save matches. I absolutely could not afford even one match per day.

I must, at the very least, keep a few active coals alive for days at a time. This would not only require large amounts of wood but would also prevent me from sleeping soundly through the night. Good sleep was vital to my ability to think clearly and function well. Desperation, however, ignited my imagination, and I suddenly remembered the smoldering aspect of cottonwood. So the last thing I did before falling asleep each night was to say my prayers and then lay a piece of green cottonwood inside the stove. As a result, most mornings I had at least one smoldering coal in the old gold pan with which to revive the fire. This allowed me to sleep six to eight hours at night instead of getting up repeatedly to tend the fire.

Occasionally, though, regardless of my efforts, the fire died. This required using another match, which I detested doing. Eventually, it became necessary to impose a fine upon myself for negligence. I determined that allowing the fire to go out was a crime against my need to survive, and I would therefore exact a sentence upon myself of no fire for three days. However, since I was the judge, the jury, and the executioner, as well as the mayor, the governor, and even the mail carrier of this region, I sometimes looked the other way while the criminal cheated by as much as twenty-four hours. These unlawful bribes and exceptions had me worried about my supply of matches. I became obsessed with my fire-stick inventory and re-counted the dwindling stash almost every day.

One habit that I had practiced for many years was to place a booklet of matches in all of my hunting shirts. The two shirts I had with me had a combined total of nineteen paper matches. I also had a lighter. It was a life-long habit to bring a lighter on hunting trips, primarily to check the wind direction just before initiating a stalk upon prey. However, I had no clue as to how many flames a lighter could produce. I would have to guess. Since this one was only about one-fourth full of lighter fluid, I estimated that it might produce around twenty-five flames, give or take. "I should be able to start at least forty fires from this point forward," I said aloud, "but the more I conserve, the better."

So, right then I determined to "dry camp" i.e., go without fire as many days and nights as possible, regardless of the punishment game I had been playing. This would mean cooking and dry smoking enough meat to last several days at a time while at the same time melting snow for drinking water. I should be able to do both of those things at once.

Melting snow was preferred over having to purify river water by boiling it. As far as staying warm at night, the bear hide, draped over my sleeping bag, should keep me warm during most cold snaps. Time would tell. Going without fire for several days at a time may not be the most comfortable choice, but this journey wasn't about comfort. It was about surviving. It was about getting home—*alive*.

Thinking and planning ahead meant life. Living in the moment, just for today, meant death. I must be careful not to lessen my chances of escaping the Brooks by being careless. Having a well-thought-out plan and executing that plan to the best of my ability would greatly increase the odds of seeing my loved ones again.

In addition to cooking and melting snow whenever I did light a flame, I would also light a moose fat candle. If the animal fuel burned efficiently enough, it might provide a very good alternative to the cottonwood coals.

With these thoughts swirling around in my brain, I decided it was time to tackle the moose meat. I walked over to the stash and threw back the tarp. The three quarters, rib meat, liver, and heart were there as I had left them. Missing were the tenderloins and both of the long, back straps. These, my favorite portions, I had already consumed.

My plan was to slice and smoke-dry as much of the bounty as possible. The tougher portions, such as the shoulder and rib meat, would make excellent jerky, providing upwards of seventy-five to eighty pounds of chewy protein. This, combined with the rendered bear fat, would be perfect sustenance for the journey home.

The better quality sections of meat would continue to sustain me over the next two months. The two hindquarters, weighing ninety to one hundred pounds each, I left intact, but the liver and heart I sliced into small steaks. Even partially frozen, it all looked extremely appetizing.

I was tempted to put the brakes on and fry a steak right then. Even if I had to clean up the shovel and use it as a makeshift frying pan, moose steak fried in bear grease just seemed too good to resist, especially given the fact that I still had several unused packets of salt and pepper left over from the MREs.

Then suddenly, and with great delight, I recalled the MRE hot sauce! Hot sauce, one of my favorite condiments, is found in every MRE. That realization pushed me over the edge. I quickly cut a thick steak from one of the moose hams, covered the stash with the tarp, and headed straight for the shovel.

Once I had a bed of red-hot coals, I placed my newest innovation, "the miner's frying pan," on top and added a generous dollop of bear fat. Soon the grease was popping. I placed the tantalizing chunk of meat in the shovel. As it sizzled and popped, it filled the woods with a most savory smell. I sprinkled it with salt and pepper.

My mouth began to salivate. Just minutes later I was chewing a piece of what seemed at the time to be the best steak I had ever cut with a knife. Wow! Then I added the hot sauce and my taste buds went into orbit. Now *that* was a morale booster!

In all the culinary excitement, I almost forgot to multitask with the match I had used. Hurriedly, I added spruce twigs to the dying embers, built up a healthy fire once more, and melted snow until the saucepan was full of water. Next, I melted some moose fat in the shovel and poured it into the birch bark cup. I lay a piece of 550 cord in the grease, lit one end of it, and placed it in the cave. That was my first experiment with an oil candle.

Sleep ambushed me while I stared at the little flame.

When I awoke the next morning, to my delight, the wick was still burning. Now I had at least two ways to conserve matches.

By late afternoon, the rib and shoulder meat was sliced into strips and ready for smoking, one rear quarter had been cut into thick steaks and roasted, and the other quarter I left uncut. The moose and bear fat got rendered to a versatile substance to be used for cooking, food, or candle fuel.

I celebrated that night with a piece of fried moose liver smothered in hot sauce.

My celebration was short-lived, however, as I needed to gather more firewood. Now that my sustenance was secured, I needed to gather food for the fire. With daylight decreasing by seven minutes every twenty-four hours, finding wood became a challenge.

I spent the daylight hours of the next three days searching for, cutting, breaking, and hauling more firewood to the cave. With the shortened days, this amounted to about fourteen hours of total work time but resulted in almost seven hundred pieces of wood. I was meticulously counting and calculating. That meant I had a supply that would last at least a month if I followed my fire conservation plan, which included a mix of cottonwood and candles.

Physically, I was getting tired again. The strain of the task was not made easier by the deepening snow. Yet I could've endured another day or two of chopping, hauling, and stacking had I not been so mentally sick of it.

I sat on the stump in front of the cave and contemplated the wearisome cycle in which I found myself: I would work until I was mentally and physically exhausted, eat a big feast, rest a few hours, and then return to the grind until I collapsed again. I was trapped in a rat race, just as if I were back in civilization. I had always blamed the city life, but maybe the blame rested upon my own shoulders. It seemed as though there should be a better way.

Slowly, I contemplated the prescription for work and rest given in the Bible. From the very beginning, God Himself had rested on the seventh day. My dad used to say,

"God didn't rest because He was tired. He rested that He might enjoy His creation."

God commanded man in the Old Testament to rest one day out of every seven. Even though we are not commanded to do so in the New Testament, I suspected there must be some advantages to following this divine prescription. Resting on Sunday had been my family's tradition when growing up. But somewhere along life's way, I had allowed that habit to fall by the wayside. Maybe now would be a good time to reintroduce the practice into my schedule.

Since the plane crash, however, I had lost track of which day of the week it was. Regardless, I simply and suddenly decided that tomorrow I would break out of this vicious cycle and begin the observance of a "Sabbath" for the physical and even the spiritual benefits. True to my word, I spent the next day sleeping in late, cooking tea, eating a big brunch, and reading Scripture. I made it a point not to worry, fret, or even think about survival on this day of rest.

Whenever I found myself beginning to calculate, inventory, or imagine the dangers of the journey home, I would force my mind to think about something more pleasant, more peaceful. Stress, after all, is mostly in the mind. If I could control my mind, peace would follow. And the greatest peace is found in God. "You will keep him in perfect peace, whose mind is stayed on You" [Isa. 26:3].

The most rigorous thing I did that day was skip rocks across the river. The reward was immediate. That self-imposed Sabbath was so enjoyable, so very relaxing, that I wondered why I hadn't rediscovered the tradition years ago. I was renewed in every way.

At that moment, I determined that, whether or not I ever escaped the wild, I would continue practicing this tradition for the remainder of my days. It had completely recharged my mind, body, and soul. As darkness descended, I crawled inside the cave, eased into the bag, pulled the bear rug over my head, and quietly sang myself to sleep.

— 10 —
The Chaga

As my survival-needs list grew shorter, my "frills list" grew longer. Once the absolute necessities such as food, water, shelter, and fire were met, I began to miss some of the little extras normally taken for granted in civilization. The most desired item missing in my supplies was coffee. Oh, how I craved the heavenly nectar! Knowing there was no way to obtain such a thing hundreds of miles from any store, I had to continually shove the desire to the back of my mind and settle for the various teas nature provided: Rosehip with a sprig of spruce needle was healthy but not delectable. Blueberry with a touch of cranberry was very healthy as well as tasty. Fortunately, I still had a few packets of MRE sugar, which helped the tea taste even better, but even that little touch of home was almost gone.

In an extreme survival situation, when one is living on the edge of life and death every day, little things like hot tea, rendered bear fat, or an old rusted-out woodstove make a huge difference.

While pondering these things, I was poking the campfire and staring at my pile of freshly cut wood. Subconsciously, I began to focus on a growth on the side of one of the cottonwood logs. At first, the thing that captured my gaze had not yet registered in my mind. However, when it finally did, I screamed like a girl—

"AAEEEH!" The sudden outburst startled me. For a split second, I had no idea why I had been overtaken by such an involuntary outburst. Then it dawned upon me: I WAS LOOKING AT COFFEE! Of course it wasn't exactly Yirgacheffe or French Riviera, but it was definitely true-to-life, one hundred percent, ALASKAN WILDERNESS COFFEE, GROWING ON THE SIDE OF A PIECE OF PUNKY 'OLE COTTONWOOD! My eyes were bulging out of my head. My brain was racing, trying to comprehend the miracle attached to the chunk of wood, just feet away. Sure enough, it was a pumice about the size of my fist that, if ground up, could be used as a coffee substitute.

I never would've been able to identify this fungus were it not for my good friend Glenn. A biologist for the Alaska Department of Fish and Game, Glenn had given me a mug of what I thought was hot cider while visiting in his home last year. Upon tasting it, however, I had to enquire, "What is this? It's pretty good."

"It's Chaga," he said, with a big grin underneath his drooping mustache. "It's actually a mushroom type fungus that grows on the sides of deciduous trees, mostly birch and cottonwood. At first glance, it looks pitch black and very rough, like a piece of coal," he continued. "If you take a closer look, however, the top half is black; the bottom half, brown. Alaskan natives and sourdoughs have used it to make a healthy tea for generations. They grind it to powder and use it like you would instant coffee. It is very high in antioxidants and carbohydrates. It also provides a chemical to the brain SIMILAR TO CAFFEINE."

Upon recalling this last statement, I could hear Glenn's voice almost audibly. No wonder I screamed like a girl! This was one of my greatest finds out here on the edge of nowhere. "My, how God provides!" I exclaimed—and screamed like a little girl again! I stood to my feet and shouted, "Thank you, Lord!" This providentially provided treat really lifted my spirits, to put it mildly. It was just another example, another 'evidence' that God was watching over me and cared about even the little things.

It brought to mind the time when my friends Neal and Ernie and I were brown-bear hunting out of Larsen Bay on Kodiak Island. I had been drawn by Alaska's lottery system for spring brown bear. We hired a boat captain to take us down the shoreline about ten miles. While motoring to our hunting camp, we asked our transporter whether or not we should have brought any fishing gear. He responded in the negative since it was too early yet for the king salmon run. We were comforted by his answer because that had been our assumption as well. So, in order to minimize the amount of gear, we hadn't bothered to bring any fishing poles or tackle.

Once we got settled into our campsite, however, we immediately began to notice some jack kings[8] swimming in the crystal clear waters of the bay, near the mouth of a freshwater creek. After kicking ourselves for not following our gut instinct to bring at least *some* fishing gear, we forgave and forgot until the next day.

We had just come back to camp after a long morning hunt when we spotted a seal chasing one of these early return king salmon about one hundred feet from shore. The water was so transparent that we were able to enjoy the entire drama as it unfolded. The seal caught the king, bit its heart out, played with it for a while, eventually lost interest, and swam away. Well, we thought this very cool wilderness drama had ended until a few hours later when, at low tide, we discovered a freshly killed king salmon lying delicately on the rocks and seaweed as if placed there by an Alaskan chef for our consumption. My friends and I were so delighted that we actually danced a hillbilly jig around the fish!

For the next two nights, we enjoyed salmon steaks, savoring every bite and grinning from ear to ear. We were careful to give thanks. We felt like the Old Testament prophet Elijah, whom God fed by sending ravens to his campsite. The only difference in our case was that God used a seal instead of a bird.

Well, God's provision in this vast wilderness had surprised me once again. Even though I certainly didn't need coffee or Chaga to survive, it was just one of those comforting reminders that God is present in every situation and that He is in control whether we realize it or not—whether we believe it or not. One of my favorite authors and theologians of years gone by, A.W. Pink, said in his book *Elijah*, "It is only our lack of faith that we do not see the hand of God in every circumstance." How true, I thought, as I recalled this quote. If God is aware of and in control of every leaf and sparrow that falls, truly He knows and cares about us and our needs and even our desires.

The next morning, with great anticipation, I pierced the fungus with my knife, broke it apart, and then began cutting it into slivers. It was quite hardened for a mushroom-type plant but softer than wood. The texture was very rough. I placed the shavings on

_____

[8] A jack is an immature king salmon that has returned to its spawning grounds early; therefore, it is smaller than but just as delicious as a full-grown fifty or sixty pounder.

a flat stone and used another stone to grind it. I needed to create as much surface area as possible so that the water could not only pick up more of the flavor of the pumice but also absorb whatever caffeine-like chemical it possessed. Eventually, I ended up with a very coarse powder mixed with small shavings. I then added a fistful of the raw pumice to my mug of water and slow-boiled it for five minutes. I moved it a few inches from the fire and let it steep a while. This produced sixteen ounces of wilderness java. Nervously, I held the mug of brew in my gloved hands, waiting on the edge of the metal cup to cool.

Would the crudely processed growth taste as good as it had at Glenn's house? Would it be a reasonable substitute for the coffee I so greatly longed for? Finally, I could wait no more and slowly brought the steaming liquid towards my mouth. I licked my dry, cracked lips, softly blew the steam away, and sipped with my eyes closed.

It was as heavenly as a first kiss.

Unlike a kiss, it tasted earthy, but in a good way. It also had a slightly nutty sweetness to it. To be precise, it didn't taste much like coffee, but the thought that it possessed anything related to caffeine was all I needed to know in order to enjoy it. Considering I was, for all practical purposes, stranded in this rugged wilderness purgatory, finding such a treasure was quite the miracle. I placed the remainder of the Chaga in my pack and looked forward to enjoying more of it later. From that day forward, I was always on the lookout for the pumice and was able to harvest at least one or two per week.

— 11 —
THE CRISIS

The days passed like clouds and winter intensified. The cold, combined with wind, became brutal. The wind didn't just chill the bones; it burnt the flesh. Because of the severity of the weather, I found myself backsliding on my "no fire" plan more and more frequently. Eventually, I tailored the grizzly blanket into a cape and wore it as such throughout the day but covered up with it at night. This was the only way I could venture outside or survive the nights without fire. In addition, I rigged a crude curtain across the mouth of the cave using the moose blanket. This greatly hindered the extremely cold and heavy air from pouring into my dwelling. Since cold air acts much like water, it flows downhill and seeks the lowest point. Anything done to hinder this movement helps. The harder the frigid air has to work to get to you, the better.

The amount of time I was forced to stay in the shelter greatly increased as the daylight and temperatures decreased. My wood supply dwindled far more rapidly than I had anticipated. The thermometer on my backpack had bottomed out several weeks ago, so all I could do was guess. Based upon my experience of over forty winters in Alaska, I surmised it was between -25 and -30 degrees Fahrenheit. However, I knew the weather could easily change in just a matter of hours.

One of two factors could improve my current situation. If clouds moved in, the cover would hold in heat and raise the temperature. Or a chinook[9] would do the same. Barring either one of these occurrences, however, the weather would steadily worsen. If the skies remained clear, it could easily drop to -40 or even -50 in this region.

---

[9] A chinook is what Alaskans call the warm, Japanese current that occasionally sweeps across Alaska and raises the temps dramatically. I've seen the temperature rise by as much as eighty degrees overnight.

Most people find it hard to believe there is a noticeable difference between -25 and -50. However, once it has been -50 for a week or two, -25 actually feels noticeably *warmer* for sure. Even so, -25 was just too cold to venture very far from the cave in search of firewood. I'd have to hope and pray for warmer temps before I could safely exit. In addition, the wind was a constant added curse. Not only did the wind chill greatly increase the chances of freezing to death, but the dreaded whiteout it created made it impossible to realize any sense of direction.

I was in no hurry to become hopelessly separated from my shelter. I decided, as long as I had wood for the stove, oil for the lamp, and food for my body, I'd sit tight and pray for better conditions. If the wood supply ran dry, I'd just have to rely on the little bit of heat from the lamp and tough it out.

I had been keeping track of the days by notching my walking stick. Now, after two long weeks of miserable cold and wind, I was stir-crazy. It was becoming an extreme mental and emotional challenge. Once again, my world had shrunk from the vast expanse of Alaska to a very tiny space. That fact, combined with drastic loss of daylight, made the psychological challenge unbearable.

From the time of the crash, which I estimated to be seven or eight weeks earlier, to now, I had lost at least four hours of sunshine. Daybreak at this latitude at the end of October wasn't until 10:00 a.m. Sunset was at 3:00 p.m. The darkness was turning out to be my greatest battle. Not only was I greatly limited in what I could accomplish outside, but I was also becoming drained psychologically and emotionally.

The barrel stove, the wood, the animal hides, and the sleeping bag would protect me from the cold, no matter how severe. The meat I had harvested and the fat and the berries would protect me from starvation. The melted snow and hot tea would protect me from dehydration. The good 'ole .454 Casull would protect me from predators (at least for two more volleys). But nothing could protect me from the darkness of the Arctic and the confinement of the cave except my own mind and spiritual condition. The mental and spiritual strength I would need to fend off my own depression, brought on by events I could not control, would have to come from God. I would read my Bible, pray, sing, and exercise. The rest, well—the rest was in His hands. Right about then, I remembered one of my mother's favorite songs and began to sing in the darkness:

> I don't know about tomorrow;
> I just live from day to day.
> I don't borrow from its sunshine,
> For its skies may turn to gray.
> I don't worry o'er the future,
> For I know what Jesus said.
> And today I'll walk beside him,
> For He knows what is ahead.
>
> Many things about tomorrow
> I don't seem to understand,
> But I know who holds tomorrow,
> And I know who holds my hand.[10]

I crawled deeper into my sleeping bag still humming the tune. Soon, my voice trailed off into the rhythmic breathing of sleep. And the animals rejoiced.

My hopes for awaking to a bright and beautiful day were dashed before I even opened my eyes. I could hear the wind like a runaway train, crashing through the valley. Robert Service described it in his famous poem *The Cremation of Sam McGee*: "And the heavens scowled, and the huskies howled, and the wind began to blow."

I tried to fall back to sleep, to give the day a second chance, but all I could hear was nature's locomotive barreling down upon my cave. "Wow! Now that's a storm!" I said in my gravelly morning voice. Shivering, I hurriedly dressed, stoked the fire, relieved myself outside, and then re-secured the meat cover by adding heavier rocks. Because of the windblown snow, the boulders weren't difficult to find but were almost impossible to dislodge. After great physical

---

exertion, I succeeded in placing three heavy ones on the tarp.

Once back inside the shelter, I alternated between peace and terror. Things would calm outside for a few short minutes, but then the storm and my fearful imaginations would begin all over again. I felt as though each time the winds abated, it was just so the mountains could take a deep breath and then exhale with greater ferocity.

During the brief lulls, I'd hurry outside, search like a madman for firewood, cling to as many sticks and wood chunks as possible while running, slipping, falling, and, finally, sliding back into the cave like a baseball player trying to score the winning run. Sometimes I made it back with an armful; sometimes, with just a stick in each hand. As hurried and dangerous as these brief excursions were, they helped me stay sane. The fresh air, the exercise, the panic, and the ensuing adrenaline rush it produced actually began to mimic a sporting event, a game against the elements. To be sure, it was a very serious contest between the storm and me, but it was one I believed I could win as long as I avoided a broken leg.

After five more grueling days—a total of almost three weeks— Mother Nature's temper abated and with it, the deadly cold and winds. I was ecstatic. Once again, I had emerged victorious following a major battle with the Brooks Range. Finally, I could exit safely, exercise without risk, and soak up sunshine, air, space "…and freedom!.." I yelled as loudly as possible.

Trees were down all across the landscape. The area as far as I could see was either covered with very deep snowdrifts or completely barren, windswept. There was no in-between.

But I was still alive and kickin'. This was cause for a barbecue celebration. Since I had by now enjoyed so much of the moose, I decided to give the griz a try.

Skeptical, yet rife with anticipation, I sliced off a thick frozen bear steak and soon had a campfire blazing. I set the chunk of meat just close enough to the fire to thaw it. Once thawed, I skewered it with a stout green willow stick and held it almost on top of the bed of red-hot coals. Even though I cooked it more thoroughly than I would have a beef or moose steak, it still didn't take long before I had a medium-well grizzly bear porterhouse smack dab in front of me. I couldn't wait any longer and chanced a bite.

The result really surprised me! I fully expected to taste it and then react by slinging it as far as possible from my kitchen. Instead, it was quite delectable and reminded me of a big, juicy black bear chop. Upon being reminded of black bear meat, an old but sweet memory began emerging from the fog of my mind and with it, a recipe.

Many years ago, my wife and I were traveling north of Fairbanks on the remote Elliot Highway. We decided to stop and say hello to some homesteader friends who ran a little grocery store and gas station about fifty miles up the road. Well, our timing could not have been better because Joe and his wife, Nancy, were just setting dinner on the table.

"Please join us," they cheerfully invited.

"We haven't seen anyone from town in so long, and we're behind on all the news. So what's happening with you folks and the outside world?"

While we were reporting all the updates in our lives and around town, a beautiful pot roast in a cast iron kettle was set before us.

"That looks delicious," my wife gleefully expressed. "Is it moose?"

"Nope, not today. Last night a passerby hit a small black bear right down the road, and rather than see it go to waste, we butchered it. This roast is one of the hindquarters."

"Oh my, it's a good thing we're hungry," I thought and my eyes met my wife's skeptical gaze.

We said grace and then, with the entire wilderness family of mama, daddy, and eight children watching, we bravely partook.

The first thing I noticed was how tender the meat was; secondly, how rich the dark mushroom and onion gravy was; and thirdly, how *delicious* it was!

I spoke without thinking: "Wow, this is way better than I expected!"

Immediately, my poor embarrassed wife stretched her leg underneath the table and lightly kicked me.

"Ouch! What was that for?" I whined.

Everyone, especially the kids, burst into laughter. I felt my face turn red. Not only was our hostess gracious by not prolonging my embarrassment with her remarks, but she also depressurized the moment by offering me some of her homemade cranberry catsup. I accepted readily for more reasons than one, and as soon as I tasted it, my eyes widened with enthusiasm for the second time in less than a minute.

"Wow again!" I exclaimed.

"This red sauce just took an already delectable dish and put it over the top. This is absolutely the *best* meat and condiment combination I've *ever* had in my life!" I exclaimed. And I meant it.

Later that night, my wife said she got a kick out of my "best ever" comment at the dinner table.

"You may have gotten a *figurative* kick," I replied, "but I got the *literal* kick!"

"Yes, but you plagiarized my saying," she teased; "you're always making fun of me for saying 'that's the best ever' about everything, and now you're saying it."

"Yes," I replied, "but when I say it, it's true." We both had a good laugh.

The recipe for the cranberry meat sauce was simple, and though I didn't have all of the ingredients with me in my current predicament, I believed I had enough of the components to come close to what was served to us years ago. I had to remain conscious, also, of conserving my supply of berries. Their primary purpose was for nutritious, hot tea. However, I felt that for this one, big celebration, the use of a small handful of the wilderness fruit was justified.

Carefully, I put one-fourth cup of cranberries in my tin mug, contributed about half a packet from the last of the sugar, and then added a little salt, pepper, and hot sauce. (The recipe actually called for vinegar but, having none, I happily used the hot sauce.) I then added about three tablespoons of warm water, mixed the ingredients thoroughly, and "WALLAH," I had my delicious cranberry catsup. The only missing ingredients used by my homesteader friend were raw honey and garlic powder. Even so, it was almost as good as I remembered it being twenty-five years ago, and it *really* complimented the griz steak.

The surprisingly savory meat, seasoned with just a touch of salt and pepper and dipped in the spicy cranberry sauce, ignited an absolute taste-bud explosion in my mouth. Every bite was as tender as any pork chop I had ever eaten. Out of sheer joy and gratitude, I gave thanks to God *before* and *after* that victory feast.

Since I was already in the celebration mode, this day was easy to declare as one of my "Sabbaths"—a time to eat, rest, and meditate without worrying. I rejected any and all stressful thoughts. I knew the beautiful, enjoyable days would soon be outnumbered by the nightmare days, so I made a conscious decision to avoid work and stress, if just for a day. My brain, body, and soul needed the respite.

The next day, however, I jumped right back into the fray of survival tasks and began cutting more wood, melting more snow, rendering moose fat, gathering what few stranded berries remained, and re-securing my meat stash.

I became so preoccupied that darkness fell without my realizing it. After spending so many days in solitary confinement, I was overjoyed at the opportunity and ability to work outside. The crisp night air, the moonlit landscape, and the darkness above so full of twinkling stars spoke to my soul; then, slowly, like a piece of classical music, the Northern Lights[11] began building.

At first, they appeared as a pale green line across the distant horizon. Within just a few minutes, however, they began moving rapidly, displaying multiple colors. Blue, green, purple, and a touch of red danced across the pitch-black, star-studded canvass of the night sky. They coiled like a serpent, then stretched from horizon to horizon, gathered once again, and then waved like an enormous flag in the wind. It was a striking crescendo to a magnificent concert! With no artificial light to diffuse this vivid light show, it was stunning, and the breathtaking scene elicited subconscious praise from my lips:

---

[11] The Aurora Borealis (commonly known as the Northern Lights) is caused by huge solar explosions hurling electrically charged particles towards the earth. Upon colliding with the atmosphere, the dark sky becomes a backdrop for these breathtaking displays. The color or colors are somewhat determined by the angle at which the particles hit the atmosphere. Many times, the particles hit the lower heavens around the poles in the shape of a halo or crown. Occasionally, the halo "slips." This affords people in the northern U.S. a chance to see them. Because of the angle, these rare displays at lower latitudes are usually red. Prime time for viewing this phenomenon is in September, October, and March. I suppose that during these months, the sun must experience more violent storms. It is no coincidence that these are also the months when thousands of tourists come to Alaska hoping to see the heavenly light show.

"Truly, Lord, how great Thou art!"

A spiritual joy came over me that I had not experienced in quite a while. I could not help kneeling on the frozen ground and giving thanks to my Creator. I realized then and there that the one who made such a complex, beautiful masterpiece could surely take care of me.

Rising, I continued gathering wood in the moonlight. As I did, I whispered to myself, "God has spared my life numerous times, provided me with a 'Shelter in the Time of Storm,' given me meat for my survival, allowed me to heal from my injuries, and now has given me great comfort in this awesome demonstration of His sovereign hand. It just doesn't get any better than this!"

Then, to my pleasant surprise, it did. A pack of wolves began to howl. First one, and then several others answered. It made the hair on the back of my neck rise and my flesh tingle. Yet I was not afraid. In fact, my spoken thought was, "I would never have asked God to put me through this tragedy and trial. Yet knowing this is God's will, I wouldn't trade the experience for anything. My soul is far different from what it was almost three months ago, and I know it."

My devotional thoughts were interrupted by the barks, moans, and howls of the wolves. It wasn't frightening to me in the least. I know wolves all too well. They are, for the most part, cowards. They have an acute fear of humans. If at any time I felt threatened, one shot in their direction would scatter them like roaches surprised by light. They attack their prey only if victory is sure. Their tactic, though smart and effective, is also cruel. The pack surrounds the victim and attacks from all sides. The wolves in front are actually there to distract while the wolves in back hamstring the victim. Once this is accomplished, they either move a safe distance away until the victim drops, or, if they're really hungry, they begin to feed before the animal hits the ground. If their target is wounded or weak already, such as an injured caribou or a pregnant cow moose, that is certainly to their advantage.

However, even if their prey does not happen to be at a disadvantage when the wolves are hungry or simply in the mood to kill, they care not. A large pack is fearless. Sheer numbers give them the ability to overcome the strongest of foes, including grizzlies. Other than man, the only creature I know of in Alaska brave enough to take on a pack of wolves is the wolverine.

Once years ago, I saw a wolverine take a caribou kill from five wolves. The carcass soon to be in dispute was near a giant boulder. The wolverine had tracked the caribou for miles until the weary animal collapsed, completely exhausted. While he was feeding, a pack of wolves charged in, ran him off, and stole his prize. The wily creature observed the thieves from a safe distance and then came up with a plan. Like an angry miniature bull, he charged—spitting, hissing, and snarling.

The suddenness of the attack caught them off-guard and momentarily scattered them, allowing the wolverine to place himself in front of the great rock yet directly behind his kill. The pack of thieves was then prevented from assaulting their wise old enemy from the rear. Instead, they were forced to attack him face to face. This was way outside their comfort zone. The genius move of the wolverine wreaked havoc with the wild canines. One at a time they came at him, and one by one the demon of the woods simply rearranged their cute faces. It was a delight to see. Each of the canine gang members yelped and ran away, most of them bleeding. The last wolf in line for a facelift was smart enough not to even try. He's the only one that escaped unscathed. It was at once impressive *and* entertaining.

Fortunately for me, unless cornered or starving, wolves will run from a human on any given day. With all the animal signs I had been seeing in this area, I doubted this pack was starving. I certainly wouldn't invade their space as long as they respected mine. Besides, their deep, sad moans and howling songs added the *coup de grâce* to my evening experience. Why spoil it with a gun blast?

— 12 —
The Cry

The unexpected enemy that ambushed me was neither an animal nor a criminal on the run. There was no wilderness drama or survival crisis by which I was blindsided. Everything had been fairly status quo for someone held hostage by the Brooks Range. I expected the temperature to drop, and it did. I knew the days would become even shorter, and they did. I predicted the weather would pendulum swing from wonderful to nasty, and I was not disappointed. I even anticipated boredom, claustrophobia, and a little depression as the winter progressed. My expectations were all unfolding, right on schedule. In addition, I had been provided by the good Lord all the food, shelter, and clothing I needed until I could cross the rivers and tundra and make it home. So I felt quite secure in my current condition and situation. That is, until one particular day. Interestingly enough, it wasn't even a cloudy day.

My normal routine was very simple: Sleep as late as possible since daylight didn't arrive until almost 11:00 a.m. Upon waking, stoke the remaining coals to a fire, dress, melt snow, make hot tea or Chaga, and eat. Then, step outside, away from the cave, to relieve myself. Next, gather wood, check the meat stash, pray, sing out loud, and then read all five chapters of 1 John. All these things I did every day. However, one particular day felt different. Before I even opened my eyes, I felt strangely empty . . . of everything. I wouldn't even have exited the cave at all except for the urge to relieve myself. Upon doing so, I had absolutely no desire, no motivation to do anything. I felt dead. I did not want to eat, drink, walk, sing, pray, or . . . even breathe. It was more than fatigue. I felt heavy, like my bones and blood were made of lead. My soul was as lifeless as a piece of wood.

Soulless, mindless, careless, lifeless—all these numb characteristics hit me at once. A very deep sadness descended upon my mind and, surprisingly, my body. Is this cabin fever? I wondered. "Oh boy," I groaned. "I thought I was prepared for this." Yet, I was not. No one, I concluded, could anticipate such intense inner darkness, such painful depression. The mental and spiritual cloud became so heavy, so literally heavy, that at times I just lay outside in the snow for hours, oblivious to my surroundings and the environment.

Is this really cabin fever or is something else taking place? I wondered. Whatever it is, it is absolutely unbearable! I cried without tears. I prayed without words. I tried to sing, to hum, to whistle a cheerful tune, but no music could be found anywhere in my being. My lips moved but no sound could be heard—nor did I care. Doubt flooded my heart. I doubted my relationship with God. I doubted my chances of escaping the Brooks. I doubted my health, my motives, my family, and my future. I doubted doubt itself. Guilt followed closely. Like a dismal duet of miserable companions, they taunted me. I had experienced doubt and felt guilty many times before this, but never had these two hollow-eyed tormentors been so personified. I thought of the guy named Christian in Bunyan's *The Pilgrim's Progress*. Haunted by the guilt of the past, every error I had ever made, every sin I had ever committed, piled on my conscience and brought me low, lower than I'd ever been.

For the next two weeks, I detested food and simply nibbled to survive. I'd go several days at a time with just a few bites of moose jerky or frozen berries. I ate snow but had no desire even to build a fire, much less to make hot tea or grill a steak. My faith was precarious, at best. Over and over, I asked God to help me, to make His presence known. "Where are you?" I asked. "Why is my soul cast down?" Where is the God of my salvation?" I begged for forgiveness, cried out for strength, pled for reassurance from above, all without faith or passion.

One harshly cold day, while hovering inside the bag under the bear hide, I recalled the account in Matthew's Gospel of our Lord's time of great testing in the wilderness and how, even though it was Satan who tempted the Lord Jesus, it was the Holy Spirit who led Him into the wilderness to be tempted. Deep down, I believed the Holy Spirit was my Friend, my Comforter, my Teacher, because God's Word said so. But at that moment, my struggle was whether or not to place my confidence in my feelings or in the Bible. Was this my time of proving? I'm sure it was. Did the Holy Spirit bring me to this place? I'm sure He did. But where was my comfort? Where was my strength? Where was my victory in all this? Hadn't I suffered enough?

Then I remembered that our Lord was tested forty days. I was unworthy. He was blameless. Why should I complain? Presently, though, the wicked one seemed closer than my Lord. "I cling to Christ," I whispered over and over, and then I began to quote Psalm 8: "O Lord, our Lord, how excellent is Your name in all the earth, you have set Your glory above the heavens . . ." Finally, I slept.

I was losing weight, lots of it. The symptoms of dehydration were also evident. My physical strength had dwindled down to almost nil. My mental, emotional, and spiritual condition was worse. Even though I had never contemplated taking my own life, there were many moments over the course of several days that I didn't care whether I lived or died. Dying would certainly be easier than enduring one more of these torture sessions. Had a wandering winter bear come my way, I honestly believe I would have offered myself to him. Many nights I dreamt of my demise, without fear. Instead of waking up in a cold sweat, I awoke, *disappointed* to be alive.

"There are times when all you can do is hang on," my native friend Roy used to say. Roy was a highly respected elder in the Ahtna tribe. He had been through great tragedy himself when he lost his dear wife of forty-five years in a horrible accident. Even though that crisis is what God used to answer his wife's prayers and bring Roy to accept and believe in Christ, he was in agony of soul for a long time. We spent much time praying and crying together. As a result of his very personal journey through the valley, Roy was one person I considered to be an expert in suffering. His words of wisdom now came to mind. "Roy," I mumbled from under the griz hide, "I'm hangin' on, I promise, I'm hangin' on . . . but barely."

Little did I realize my epic crisis of the soul was about to end—with a bang.

In a rather ironic way, my nemesis of the north saved me. My old enemy from weeks ago showed his gnarly face again—the wolverine. I was about fifty yards from the cave, stumbling around, half dazed, half searching for wood, when I spotted the old wolverine headed straight for my meat stash. As depressed and apathetic as I was, this I could not ignore.

Suddenly I felt an emotion, and it startled me! The ability to actually *feel* surprised me more than the reappearance of the wily thief. It was slight, but resentment smoldered in my soul like a cottonwood ember. Had he come around a few days earlier, I probably would've just given up, lain down on top of the blue tarp, and let him chew on me awhile. Maybe I had been improving so slowly that I didn't realize it until now. This critter awakened something deep within that I hadn't felt in three miserable weeks.

As I looked more closely, my suspicions were confirmed. It was the same animal that had chased me up the tree a month earlier. He had the characteristic limp from his missing paw, his tail was gone, and he sported the same battle-worn face. Hoping this would not be a repeat of our first encounter, I made my presence known by shouting insults and waving my arms. With great disdain, he completely ignored me just as he had when we last parted ways. "That's fine, you rude thief," I mumbled. "This time, I have a nice little surprise for you." Then I realized I didn't. The surprise was on me.

I didn't have my weapon with me! Though I had been carrying it with me consistently since our first encounter, lately I'd had absolutely no concern for my well-being—until now. Fortunately, this time, the creature seemed so focused on the meat that he paid no attention to me. Slowly I walked a half circle around him, made my way to the shelter, and quickly grabbed my firearm. I double-checked the chamber and headed straight for him. By this time, he was sniffing, biting at, and pulling the tarp that covered my moose and grizzly meat. Not really wanting to kill the crusty critter, I started to spend my next-to-the-last round by shooting in his direction. After calculating the value of my last two rounds of ammo, I hesitated but quickly chose to shoot. The food stash was of greater importance than the bullets. Still, I thought I'd try yelling first.

"HEY YOU OLD VARMIT, GET AWAY FROM THERE!" I screamed. That'll spook him all the way to Canada, I thought. But, to my shock and dismay, he didn't even look up. I wasn't even twenty yards away! Could it be this fur-covered devil was so ancient that he was deaf?

I pointed the gun just over his head. BOOM! The explosion was deafening. Again, he didn't even look up. There I stood in disbelief with just one bullet and one option left: if I wanted to defend my meat supply, I must shoot to kill. But I honestly did not want to terminate this wilderness warrior's life. "You're really goin' soft, man," I scolded myself.

Desperate to appease my conscience, I instantly came up with at least three reasons this intruder needed to die:

(1) He was very old and decrepit and most likely wouldn't survive the winter.

(2) His fur could help insulate my hunting boots.

(3) He was chewing on my moose meat!

Quickly, I circled behind him, stalked within twelve yards, and then aimed center of mass. Suddenly, he turned his head and looked back at me, providing me with a perfect quartering away shot. Like a lunatic, his eyes pierced mine. He snarled, and in so doing, displayed his last remaining tooth for the last time. BOOM!

The impact of the 440-grain bullet picked up the fifty-pound animal and catapulted him several yards beyond my groceries. To say it was overkill is an understatement, but it isn't like I had a choice of weapons. I considered it both merciful and appropriate to conclude his long and fierce life by using a handgun big enough to kill an elephant.

I sat down a while, waiting for my ears to stop ringing. There was blood splatter in the snow from the point of impact all the way to the carcass. After a full minute, I slowly and respectfully approached the 'ole boy and knelt down beside him. The exit hole was the size of a tennis ball.

"I know we had our differences, you 'ole coot but I couldn't let you steal my food. Besides, you know how you boys like to pee all over everything. I promise, though, I won't let you go to waste, and every time I use your fur, or what's left of it, I'll remember you with respect."

Even though the wolverine pelt would be quite valuable to my survival, I felt saddened. It wasn't like I had lots of company around here. Sometimes even bad company was better than none, especially if they didn't stay long. Ironically, it was this mixture of excitement, anger, and sadness that snapped me out of the deadly depression I had been in for so long. Not until I had finished skinning the carcass did it hit me that the cabin fever, or whatever it was that had plagued me for the past three weeks, was gone. Evidently, this startling confrontation with a viable threat to my survival had forced me out of the pit of despair.

After skinning the carcass, I spent the brief sunlight hours of the next two days fleshing, stretching, and smoke-tanning the pelt just as I had the others, only this time, I applied a little more TLC. After all, I had made a promise to the worn-out warrior. This hyper-warm fur would turn a pair of fall hunting boots into insulated winter footwear and none too soon. Except for one extra pair of wool socks and one pair made of cotton, all my others were in pitiful shape. I could now line the inside of my footgear with some of the warmest fur known to man.[12]

As a result of my poor appetite of late and ensuing weight loss, I had just enough extra space inside my boots to accommodate my new, very comfy boot liners. While trying them out, I couldn't help shaking my head at the way God had once again provided. The Lord brought that feisty creature full-circle to help me in my greatest time of need. The storm that had raged inside of me was over. My heart, my soul, and my passion for surviving had returned, *and* I had warm footgear for the journey home.

That night, under the stars, I sat by the campfire and began to sing:

> In the dark of the midnight have I oft hid my face,
> While the storm howls above me, and there's no hiding place.
> 'Mid the crash of the thunder, precious Lord, hear my cry,
> Keep me safe till the storm passes by.
> Till the storm passes over, till the thunder sounds no more,
> Till the clouds roll forever from the sky;

---

[12] The native peoples of the north highly prize wolverine fur because it repels moisture, thus providing a frost-free "ruff." The ruff is the fur around the edge of the parka hood, closest to the face.

Hold me fast, let me stand in the hollow of thy hand,
Keep me safe till the storm passes by.[13]

---

[13] "Til the Storm Passes By" by Thomas Mosie Lister. © 1973, renewed 2001 Mosie Lister Songs (admin. by Music Services) / Southern Faith Songs (admin. by Music Services) All rights reserved. BMI. Used by permission.

— 13 —
THE CARGO

It was early December. The lakes, ponds, and rivers were frozen. My trek to the road could begin any day. Soon I would be breaking trail to freedom. The prospect of being able to cross the rivers made going home finally seem like a reality. My enthusiasm grew with each passing day. Thanks to moose meat, bear meat, and bear fat, I began reclaiming some of my weight. Now I needed strength and stamina. It was time to start training for the escape.

The distance from the cave to the river was about one hundred yards. I started an exercise routine that began with power walking—one trip to the river's edge and then back to the shelter. Every day I added a couple of laps. Within a week, I could do the routine with ease, so I doubled the number of laps, increased the speed at which I traveled, and took on the daypack. This, along with lots of protein, Chaga, and tea, soon had me in good shape.

On the last day of physical training, I added my sleeping bag and pelts to the equation. Upon performing the task with ease, fully loaded, I knew I was ready. The next day, I'd observe my day of rest and then take inventory, pack, and hit the trail.

Feeling stronger than I had in years, I was more than ready for "take off." Of course, once I abandoned the cave and ventured beyond my exercise trail, I'd be challenged by snowdrifts, tundra, alder patches, and many other obstacles. Dark, cloudy nights would be my greatest hindrance, and windstorms and leads[14] my greatest threats. Many mushers and snow machine drivers have died from falling into a lead. Most of the time, open water can be detected by the steam that rises from it. This is due to the fact that the water temp is warmer than the air. However, when traveling in the dark, I

---

[14] Leads are what dog mushers call patches of open water on lakes and rivers during winter.

may not have the added warning this natural occurrence provides. Clear, moonlit nights would potentially provide me with extra hours of travel time but would come with added risks, low visibility being one of them. I must be patient and wise every moment. The journey would not only be demanding physically, but it would also tax me mentally.

My schedule of tasks was growing.

I needed to dry-smoke more meat. In addition, I needed to trim, smoke, and beat the bear hide again. Not only did it need reconditioning, but it was also too large for the journey. My plan was to craft it into a poncho so that I could both wear it when traveling and cover myself with it at night.

The hide was waterproof if it warmed up and rained.[15] Additionally, it would add much-needed insulation around me when the temps dropped dangerously low.

To make it useful as a poncho, however, required some extra trimming. I would also need to cut a hole in the center for my head and one on each side for my arms. The entire thing probably weighed close to twenty pounds even though I had already greatly reduced its overall size when I removed it from the bear.

The partial moose hide, grizzly hide, daypack (which contained mostly dry-smoked meat), sleeping bag, pistol, and hatchet easily weighed an estimated fifty-five to sixty pounds combined. I must gauge my load carefully. Deciding what to take and what to leave was constantly on my mind. All this and more took hours of preparation and hours of planning. My previous plan to depart within two days of feeling physically prepared, I now realized, was overly optimistic.

"That's O.K." I preached. "You've waited this long; if it takes a few extra days to adequately prepare, so be it. Just get it right!"

Each night, I'd lie awake trying to anticipate every possible need, every emergency, every survival tool I might wish I had once I left my fortress. In some ways, I would miss this place of safety, but I knew that in order to see my family again, I had to take some

---

[15] I have seen it rain in December as a result of the Japanese wind current called chinook.

mighty big risks. The reward, however, so outweighed the risks that the daunting wilderness ahead seemed a trifle. I had to force myself not to think about home too much, or I might just start running like a crazy man for the Dalton Highway. This, of course, would be suicide.

Finally, my last night in the cave was upon me. It was mid-December. I was anxious, so very anxious, and excited. It had taken me a few more days than I had anticipated to get organized and accomplish everything on my survival list. The darkness was nearing its zenith, and soon daylight would begin to increase. The increase, however, would be minimal: only about a minute per day the first few days. "I guess gaining a minute a day is better than losing one," I grumbled.

My patience was finally spent. I had been relegated to this tiny dungeon for too many days. As protective as it was, I was beyond ready to escape the prison this cave and these mountains had become. It was as though the talons of the Brooks had held me in their grasp long enough. I wanted to be set free, to fly away. "Well, fly I can't; but walk—now that I *can* do!" I shouted in the night.

I awoke, as usual, to darkness. I lay there, eyes wide open, for at least two hours. Finally, a hint of light appeared on the horizon. Using the oil candle, I rummaged around, got a fire going, and made a mug of hot Chaga. I had moose jerky and bear fat for breakfast and started packing the last few items. Most of the packing I had done yesterday in anticipation of this moment.

I knelt in the snow and said a prayer of thanks and asked the Lord to keep me safe. I then quoted Psalm 27 while putting on the griz poncho. Next was the daypack, with the sleeping bag and moose hide both cinched on top. The blue tarp covered everything so that I could be seen easily from above. If I were spotted from a plane, I'd most certainly look like a giant blue tortoise.

It broke my heart, but I had to leave the now-empty and useless pistol. The behemoth weighed in at over eight pounds, counting scope and holster. I just couldn't afford the extra burden. The promise of home and loved ones made the sacrifice pale in comparison, so my gun-grief was short lived. I picked up my newly carved walking stick and never looked back, not once. The cave had been God's provision for a designated time, but now I rejected it like a mother bear rejects her young.

I followed my well-worn exercise trail to the big river and then for the first time started across its frozen surface. It had provided me with water for over three months, but now it was my bridge home—one of many I would cross over the next month.

Thankfully, my first crossing was uneventful, though a little stressful, since I was on the lookout for soft spots and leads. Once I was safely on the other side, I felt a rush of mixed emotions: I was excited to finally be moving towards home, yet I was afraid of what lay ahead. I was overjoyed at the prospect of seeing my dear family after all these months, yet anxious at the thought of how shocked they would be when I returned from the dead.

Regardless, I must press on. "Focus!" I scolded myself. "The last thing you need is tears freezing in your eyes!" That's all it took; my mind snapped to attention. I followed the drainage downstream, or south. I must move further from the highest peaks before turning east, or I would continually be faced with the impossible task of crossing mountain passes that were not only extremely steep but also choked with very deep snow drifts. My plan was to put about twenty miles between me and the Brooks and then "set my face like a flint" eastward toward the Dalton Highway.

In places, the snow was deeper than I expected. I was forced to aim for as many windswept areas as possible even though it lengthened the overall distance. Daylight faded as quickly as it had been doing for many weeks. "Gained another a minute," I said sarcastically. As my luck would have it, this was a cloudy night, so I was forced to make camp after just four hours of meandering south. No matter, by late tomorrow I should be able to turn east and march like a soldier to the road.

Curled up in my sleeping bag, moose hide under me, bear hide over me, I began to ponder: How far did I travel on my first day of escape? Accounting for all the zigzagging and detours around snowdrifts, leads, timber, and other natural obstacles, my conservative estimate was five miles. Knowing some days would be better, some worse, my overall average should be around six miles per day. If I was approximately 160-170 miles from the road, as I suspected,

I could possibly be in a warm truck, on my way home, in less than thirty days.

Thoughts like this spurred me on. Whenever I felt as though I could not take another step, I just thought about home. Whenever I felt overwhelmed by the journey ahead or the dangers around, I just thought of home. God had spared my life for a reason, and I longed to discover why. I was determined that no matter how difficult, how dangerous, or how agonizing escaping the Brooks became, I would not give up. I would not quit. Home was my destination; God was my destiny. So, in the dark I prayed, greatly anticipating daybreak, and finally fell asleep.

My second day was much like the first, including the challenge of crossing another drainage. It was about one hundred yards wide and braided. Where it joined the river I had been following, I was forced to cross. I cautiously probed the snow with my walking stick for any rotten ice, alert for any steam rising. Discovering none, I safely reached the other side, where I dropped my gear, sat on a large, frozen tussock, and began working on a piece of moose jerky.

The clouds had been breaking, so I knew the temperature would start to drop. I must choose my camp with this in mind and had just a couple of hours to do so. The predominant winds came from the northwest, so an east or southeast-facing shelter would certainly be desirable. If it became cold enough or windy enough, I'd be forced to dig a snow cave.

"Well, I'd best not stop again until I've put a few miles behind me," I mumbled as I refastened my gear and continued on. As before, I found myself continually skirting the snow drifts, always looking for the easiest route, not necessarily the shortest one. The distance this added to my journey really began to take its toll. I began thinking about snowshoes and eventually came up with a plan.

Even though crafting a pair would cost me at least a full day of travel, I'd more than make up for it if I were able to walk a much straighter line to the road. To be sure, I'd still have to dodge thick willow patches, open water, steep hills, and other obstacles; but I estimated the cumulative distance could be greatly reduced with snowshoes. This made the decision to build them easy. How to do so would be the difficult part since I had never crafted any myself.

However, I had watched an old wolf trapper make a pair several years earlier. At the time, I was interested in purchasing one of his agricultural parcels located halfway between Nenana and Healy, just off the Parks Highway. As he and I haggled over the price and sipped on what had to be some of the strongest coffee ever brewed, he crafted as good a snowshoe as I had ever seen. This was the only lesson I had in crafting winter footwear. Hopefully, I remembered enough of the process to build a pair.

As daylight faded, I spotted a large deadfall and, using my tarp and some spruce boughs, made a flimsy but sufficient one-night shelter. I threw the hides and sleeping bag inside and crawled in. That night, I fell asleep mentally fabricating snowshoes.

About an hour before noon, the pink and yellow alpine glow of December appeared on the horizon. By then, I had a small fire going, and I boiled some spruce twig tea. I held the tin cup of medicinal-tasting brew in my gloved hands and enjoyed the warmth it provided. I boiled a second cup and added small pieces of bear meat. The resulting stew was quite invigorating.

Eventually, it was light enough to see, and I began searching for green willows. They had to be just the right thickness for the framework of my snowshoes. It didn't take long to find some since willows are abundant along the rivers. I cut them, held them very close to the fire, and formed them into two elongated frames. Each frame was about fourteen inches wide across the middle, narrower at each end, and around thirty-six inches long. I chose these dimensions trusting the advice of the wolf trapper. "The long narrow ones are the best. Once, I tried those funny lookin' egg-shaped shoes," he scoffed. "They 'bout kilt me—way more hard to stay on top of the snow with them thangs. I couldn't get rid of 'em fast enough!"

Once I had the willow frames shaped correctly, I carved a couple of notches that would help secure the cord when I lashed the two ends together. I then tied several willow sticks across the inside to support the shape of the frames. Next, I scraped the hair from some of the moose hide and cut thin cords for lashing. Then I laced them back and forth across the framework. My cold fingers were aching and clumsy. Time and again I was forced to warm my hands near the fire. This delayed completion by at least a couple of hours.

The only means I had to attach the snowshoes to my boots was quarter-inch cotton rope. What remained of the military cord, I used as webbing, and I certainly could not afford to slice up any more moose hide since that was needed for insulation between my sleeping bag and the snow. I knew the cotton wouldn't stretch, so that made it my "go to" harness material. Steadily, unaware of time, I worked. I had to finish the project using campfire light, but by the time the moon arose, I had a pair of handcrafted willow snowshoes, and I was ready to break trail. The project had taken a lot of mental strength, but physically, I felt like my energy tank was full of adrenaline. That and the bright moon urged me to get going.

Soon my gear was on my back, and I was doing the zombie lunge necessary to keep from falling.

As a child, we had played "snowshoe softball." It took us a while to get the hang of running in snowshoes but once we did, the most difficult part of the game was finding the ball. We eventually solved that problem by asking Dad to paint the ball red.

Now, as I leapt forward on top of the snowdrifts, that memory brought a smile.

Unfortunately, it wasn't long before I worked up quite a sweat. This absolutely would not do. If my body became coated in perspiration, the moisture would begin to freeze as soon as I stopped moving. Hypothermia would then begin its life-threatening cycle. To prevent this, I came to a halt, removed the grizzly poncho and my hat and fastened them to my daypack along with the other things. This rearrangement had an immediate positive effect.

I must have looked like a hunchbacked Sasquatch as I half-jumped across the tundra in the moonlight.

I was forced to stop frequently, either to refasten the snowshoes or to rearrange the hardware store on my back. Though these forced pauses were frustrating, they allowed me time to cool down and further decrease the chances of perspiring. However, in spite of the pauses taken and in spite of the fact that I was traveling on a clear, cold night, I could still feel the moisture steadily increasing all over my body.

I needed to re-evaluate my situation. In the moonlight, I spotted a large spruce deadfall about twenty yards away. I rolled the burden off my back, chopped some limbs, and built a blazing fire. I lay the tarp down for flooring and removed my outer clothing. I stood as close to the fire as my face could tolerate, in my stocking feet and long johns. The steam emanated freely from my damp underclothes. It took about two hours to completely dry out. Once I crawled into the sleeping bag, I was instantly asleep and did not waken until late in the day.

"Well," I said softly, looking straight up at the sky, "that was a good trial run; now let's make some adjustments." I unzipped the bag, dressed, gathered some sticks, and rekindled the fire. By the time I finished some moose jerky stew and hot tea, I had a plan.

I would use the remaining moose hide to make a small supply sled instead of carrying everything on my back. The everything-on-the-back idea had worked until I had introduced the rigors of snowshoeing. Once that factor entered the picture, the body heat and resulting sweat generated by the task was just too much to overcome. I realized I must reconfigure my load.

By crafting a small sled, I could use the snow to my advantage. In other words, the weight of my meager yet burdensome possessions would slide over the slippery white stuff much more easily than I could carry it on my back. The snowshoes had shortened the distance but had added to the physical demands of the journey. I must counter that by getting the weight and the warmth of the gear off my back. A sled would do both and greatly increase my chances of getting to the highway alive. To *pull* fifty pounds of gear over the snow would, I surmised, be less of a strain than to *carry* fifty pounds of gear on my back.

The challenge I faced with building a sled was the lack of cordage. All of the cord had been used for snowshoe webbing, harnesses, sun-shield straps, and other projects. I had also cut as much of the moose hide as was prudent. However, I knew from listening to my native friends that willow bark could be used like twine. It was strong. It was durable. It would work.

I pulled strand after strand from the willow branches around me. The supply was limitless. It took the better part of the day but eventually, I had a one hundred percent willow framework about five feet long and just over two feet wide, with curved sides about a foot high. I then burned and scraped the remaining hair from the moose hide and stretched and tied it tightly to the frame using more willow string. The result surprised me. I had crafted a lightweight, narrow sled from nothing but what this rugged land had to offer.

After securing my burdensome gear in that beautiful, wild, homemade vehicle, I immediately realized a problem. I had no rope with which to pull the sled! "Well," I said, half scolding myself, "you shouldn't have trimmed so much of that bear hide off when you made the poncho!" Fortunately, the poncho was still a little large, but I would dearly miss its generous size at night when I needed extra warmth. "I guess I'll just have to dig a little deeper snow cave if it gets really cold," I quipped and drew my knife. I decided to cut a strip from each side, two inches wide the full length. This gave me two strips, each one two inches by seven feet. I tied one end of a strip to one front corner of the sled, the end of the remaining strip to the other front corner, and then tied the two strips together in front of my waist. Thus, I had my tow strap.

It wasn't exactly store-bought, but the result was the same: I had a strong pulling rope, only mine was crafted out of grizzly skin. As I began to tug and then to move forward with confidence, it soon became evident that this setup was going to work just fine. That narrow willow sled, covered in hairless moose hide and pulled by griz rope, almost seemed alive as it glided over the snow and ice. It took on a personality all its own and became my new partner in the wilderness. I didn't break a sweat the entire night and, other than short stops for nourishment and hydration, excitedly pressed on for the next ten hours. The wind blew, the stars came out, and the northern lights began to dance. I had never felt freer!

— 14 —
THE CORVETTE

It was at this point I turned and headed east. The tallest mountains, which had been directly behind me, were now eighteen to twenty miles to my left, or north. Even though I knew I would encounter occasional hills and valleys, they were nothing compared to the rugged, impassable sentinels of the Brooks. I had finally escaped! As long as I kept the largest peaks to my left, I knew I could keep my bearings and reach the highway.

I made good time, all things considered. The sled made a huge difference but came at a price. My first night's sleep without the moose hide underneath me was a cold one. The big tarp, folded several times with some spruce boughs underneath was better than nothing but not nearly as insulating as the moose pelt had been. After shivering most of the night, it wasn't until I was back on the trail and feeling the pull that I finally warmed up. I began to contemplate the dilemma of staying warm at night, especially since the skies had cleared and the temps were dropping.

I recalled how, years earlier, my dad had taught us kids to place a rock near the campfire and, once it got hot, to wrap it in a towel or rag and place it in our sleeping bag to keep us warm all night. It did, too. If it worked then, it would work now. The biggest unknown was how much fire-making ability I had left. It had been a while since I had checked. Right then I stopped and took inventory. Upon doing a thorough search, I was startled to find only three matches remained. The lighter was still about one-fourth full of fluid. This was not good news. I realized I had been too liberal in the use of fire in spite of my attempts to conserve. This carelessness I now regretted.

I determined from this point forward to build a fire only when I believed it to be -25 or colder. Unfortunately, I didn't have to wait long. The skies had been clear for the past couple of days, and the thermometer on my pack had bottomed out at -10 the day before. I could tell it was getting colder by the hour. A temp of -20 is obnoxious, -25 starts to hurt, and -30 and colder burns the skin, causes the facial bones to ache, and is just plain dangerous. If the mercury dropped below that, you'd better be holed up somewhere mighty cozy. Well, I could feel the burning on my face as well as on my hands in spite of the gloves. I decided that I'd better make a shelter fast and wait out this high-pressure system.

Within an hour, I located a good-size snowdrift and started digging. Careful not to work up a sweat, I took lots of breaks. Soon I had the beginning of a nice snow cave. I decided to "go the extra mile," as they say, and copy the floor plan used by a big sleeping bear we once stumbled upon while on a winter moose hunt. It happened about ten years ago.

I had applied and been drawn for a November black powder moose hunt. So the first day of the special season, we snow-machined forty miles east of the Parks Highway and then traveled a few miles up a promising valley. We parked the snow-go and climbed a small hill from which to glass for moose. We had been there just a few minutes when I began hearing (and feeling) a deep rumbling noise. At first, I attributed it to one of the U. S. Air Force bases located about fifty miles east of where we sat. There was also a smaller base about forty miles to the west. However, I began timing the rumbling noises. They were spaced evenly, at forty-five seconds apart. It took me fifteen minutes or so, but suddenly I whispered to my buddy, "Could that be a bear snoring underneath us?!"

I jumped up and began scouting the area, and sure enough, not thirty feet from where we sat on top of that snow hill was the entrance to a den! We shined our flashlights inside. A number of things immediately became apparent. First, the narrow tunnel had been used for many years. Second, about ten to fifteen feet in, it took a left turn. Third, it ended right underneath where we had been sitting. And last but not least, it was occupied by something that snored louder than an overweight Sasquatch!

Upon finding this occupied bear den, my huntin' buddy and I marveled at the ingenious method the bear had used to slow the flow of frigid air. This wise old creature had put a dogleg in the tunnel, which forced the cold air to stall a little and work harder to get to him. This bear somehow instinctively understood this principle. I was impressed enough that my curiosity was piqued, and since I had a bear tag, I crawled inside as far as I could. Eventually things just became too tight—and smelly! I snake-crawled backwards and was glad to emerge into daylight and fresh air. Since I couldn't get to him, we set up an ambush and tried to lure the snoring beast out of his den, but to no avail.

However, we must've succeeded in waking him up because the snoring stopped! After using every trick we could think of to get him to come out, I gave up.

"That hairy chicken ain't comin' out, and this hairless chicken ain't goin' back in!" I stated emphatically.

I never forgot the bear's crafty den design, and now I copied it by digging an eight-foot long tunnel, turning left almost ninety degrees, digging a little further, and concluding with a raised cul-de-sac. Once my snow shelter was complete, I crawled inside with my tarp and sleeping gear and lit the moose fat candle. The amount of heat generated by it was slight, but the inner chamber of my den soon warmed to just below freezing, even though it was far colder outside.

As nice as my arctic apartment was, I knew it would shrink by the hour. The longer the cold spell lasted, the more difficult it would be to remain in this cramped space. I'd just have to deal with it by making frequent trips outside. That shouldn't be a problem since, no doubt, nature would be calling. However, If the temperature continued to drop, I'd have to get my business done pronto, do a few jumping jacks, and get my cold carcass back inside.

I had just gotten settled in for the night when I suddenly remembered that my sled and supplies were outside, totally exposed to the rising wind. I scolded myself profusely. "You must remain mentally alert, especially at the end of a very long day such as right now! Don't relax until every task is done!" Outside, I found everything intact and breathed a sigh of relief. The wind was definitely picking up but had not yet reached hurricane force. While contemplating how to secure the sled, it suddenly dawned on me that I had a ready-made garage: the tunnel itself. Within minutes, I had reconfigured the entrance and pulled the sled three quarters of the way inside. That should secure it. An additional benefit to pulling the sled inside was that if the winds blew long enough and hard enough and sealed the exit with snow drift, all I would need to do would be to push the sled out. It would serve as my exit plow, not to mention a partial blockade to the cold.

I slept until I absolutely had to urinate. I had been resisting the urge for quite a while because I suspected Jack Freeze was waiting to ambush me as soon as I crawled outside. My suspicion was soon confirmed. The winds had obviously increased in velocity and had plugged the entrance. It took a little grunting and groaning, but finally the sled broke free and with it, a load of fresh snow. It was so cold I could hardly "go." I also had to keep one foot inside the sled to keep it from blowing away. By the time I crawled back inside and pulled the sled in behind me, my face, ears, and hands were burning. My fingers were so stiff I couldn't close them until I cupped my hands and blew on them for quite a while. I curled up like a malamute sled dog and wished for daybreak, storm break, coffee break— any kind of a break. "JUST GIMME A BREAK!" I shouted. I think I was losing it. "Get a grip," I mumbled and fell back asleep.

The weather became fierce.

I exited the tunnel only for the call of nature and believe me, she had to holler. Had there been enough room to relieve myself inside, I would've gladly done so. But there wasn't. Thus, every few hours or so, I struggled to free myself, first from the bear hide and then from the sleeping bag. Then I had to do a snake-crawl to the exit, heave-ho the sled, freeze my fanny off, perform some calisthenics, then re-enter the tunnel backwards, pull the sled in, jump in the bag, throw the griz hide on top, and shiver for ten minutes. This agonizing routine I repeated many times over the next three and a half days.

Finally, on the fourth night, the weather broke. I could tell it immediately. My snow den actually became too warm. I celebrated by sleeping outside, not under the stars but under the clouds. As beautiful as the stars and northern lights are on clear, cold nights, I strongly preferred the warmth brought in by the clouds. It was glorious.

I had slept so much the past three days that I spent the night just staring at the dark horizon, wishing for sunlight. There was no moon, or I would have been hoofin' it towards home already.

Finally, the sun had her coffee and woke up. I was waiting. The clouds were high and nonthreatening. I brushed snow off my gear, made sure everything was secure, put on my snowshoes, and broke trail for the highway.

Every day I was forced to choose to climb the hills or go around them. Those less steep, I climbed, hoping the descent was as gentle as the ascent. I had been lucky until now. After snowshoeing sideways up a gentle but long, drawn-out slope, I was shocked when I came to the edge of a cliff! I estimated the drop to be at least three hundred feet. I had to decide whether to backtrack and go around or to try another, faster route down, thus saving time and thereby daylight.

Straight ahead, the cliff's edge was sharp; the drop off, straight down. To my right and left, however, it descended at about a twelve to fifteen percent grade. I sat down, drank from my plastic water bag, chewed on a piece of jerky, and contemplated my next move.

The break was refreshing and for the moment, I felt brave. Of course, *bravery* can sometimes be a synonym for *stupidity*. At least that's the thought that flew through my mind about halfway down that hill.

In my impatience, I decided to ride the sled down the less-steep side to my right and save about two hours of backtracking. We used to sled down hills just like this as kids so, "it shouldn't be that bad," I mumbled with the confidence of an idiot.

For some odd reason, when you do things as a kid, they're fun. But those same things at forty-something are insane. For instance, most forty-six-year-olds don't T.P. their friend's yard . . . or put a potato in the exhaust pipe of their neighbor's car . . . or, as in this case, sled down a hill that has a fifteen percent grade in a sled made out of willows designed to carry just fifty pounds of gear.

I do wish these more mature thoughts had entered my mind while I was enjoying that piece of dried moose meat. But they didn't, and I nearly "bought the farm."

After removing my snowshoes and making sure everything was

tied down, I shoved off down the south edge of that hill, parallel to but about ten feet from the cliff's edge.

At first, it seemed as though the sled wasn't going to cooperate. Then suddenly it came to life—due to something called gravity. It seemed as though my gear-sled-turned-kid-rocket went from zero to sixty in five seconds, even though my top speed was probably no more than fifteen to twenty miles per hour at the peak of this near-death experience.

As the speed of my descent increased, so did the volume of my scream. The two seemed connected.

Without warning, my arctic Corvette hit a high spot on my right—probably a rock—which pin-balled the sled to the left, straight for the cliff. To be sure, the drop-off was now only about a third of what it was from the top of the hill. However, one hundred feet is still not a desirable distance to plummet. The difference between falling three hundred and one hundred feet is just whether you die quickly or slowly. That's not much comfort.

The sudden jolt sent me in a bad direction. I had to react quickly or die. I leaned right. But the sled kept going left . . . off the edge . . . and into space . . . way out into empty, frozen, space. Fortunately, I had bailed out of the death-mobile before it launched.

I rolled, slid, and with a loud "oomph!" finally plowed snow with my face and came to a stop. "Oh, that hurt! Oh, that's cold!" I had an ice-cream headache and a very sore nose, but at least I hadn't followed the path of the sled. It crashed below in dramatic fashion, judging by the aftermath. Parts, pieces, gear and willows were either scattered amongst the windswept rocks or sticking helter-skelter out of the snow. I was so glad to be alive that I momentarily forgot about the crisis I might face if any of my supplies were lost. Very quickly, though, I came to my senses and stumbled, crawled, and slid the rest of the way down the south slope. Shaken up, I hobbled around and eventually made it to the crash site. The sled was not a sled any more. Initially, I could find only a few broken willow branches. As I rummaged around, however, I breathed a huge sigh of relief when I found my daypack and, further down, the moose skin with some of the framework still attached.

My relief was short-lived, however, when I couldn't find the sleeping bag. I searched until dark and then continued searching in braille by stomping a grid, back and forth, up and down the slope, and into the flat. I poked my walking stick into an area far bigger than the crash site. Nothing. Exhausted and wet with sweat, I gave up, built a fire, dried off, wrapped up in the skins, and slept fitfully through the night.

The next day, at the peak of daylight, I began the search again. With great relief, I located the bag. It had literally rolled a hundred yards beyond everything else and jammed itself under a small sapling spruce.

Finally, I hit the trail, quite disgusted with myself.

The sled was a bust, literally. Without it, I was forced to reconfigure my supplies and place them, once again, on my back. It was necessary, also, to return to the former pattern of zigzagging around the snowdrifts. Of course, very quickly I began to overheat so I spent the next two days repairing the shoes and rebuilding the sled. I was determined to turn my latest crisis, the result of my own foolishness, into a blessing. As with the birch berry baskets, I restored everything better and stronger than before.

— 15 —
THE CONFESSION

The improved construction of the sled and snowshoes, combined with the fact that I had discarded a few items, had less food to carry, was in the best physical shape I had ever been in, and enjoyed the illumination of a full moon, resulted in great progress over the next three days and nights. Even though the combined weight of the things I had tossed or consumed (a flashlight with dead batteries, a stone I had been using to sharpen my hatchet, the binoculars, sauce pan, and the meat and bear fat that went down my gullet) seemingly did not amount to much, I knew from past experience that every ounce matters when hiking long distances.

That's a lesson I learned long ago when I first started hunting sheep. Dall sheep, as far as I'm concerned, are the greatest trophy animals in Alaska and have the best-tasting meat of any animal on earth. But it is also the most difficult Alaskan big game species to hunt. They live at high altitudes in the rugged mountains. They have eyes like an eagle. And they can navigate their territory very well. They are superior in every way to the oftentimes out-of-shape humans who hunt them. Never have I experienced an easy sheep hunt. It has always brought me to the very precipice of my physical endurance. That's why, before we board a bush plane to fly in and stalk these illusive trophies, we actually weigh every piece of gear, discard anything and everything we do not need, and count every ounce a burden because we know the terrain ahead is going to test every muscle, every tendon, every bone, and every fiber of our being.

Most experienced sheep hunters have spent at least one night on the side of a shale-covered slope, wrapped in nothing but an emergency space blanket, nursing a candle for warmth, and praying for daybreak. You may have a nicely outfitted main camp, but once you spot big daddy and set out after him, you'd best take only your weapon, pack frame, and whatever will fit in your pockets. Oftentimes, it's what you have to do if you want a big ram. That's the mentality I now had as I continued the march, once again, toward my trophy—home!

I was still chafing at my own stupidity displayed in the unnecessary sledding accident but was happy to be moving faster. I wasn't sure whether the accident was a blessing in disguise or not, but I really didn't want to take the time to figure it out. I could do that during the next forty-below spell. For now, I just needed to be moving forward while the day was bright.

Within a few hours the winds picked up and clouds blew in. The overcast skies would warm things up, but there would be no travel tonight without moonlight. I needed a cheap motel, and it wasn't long before I spotted one. It was a small rock outcrop. All it needed was a dozen or so snow blocks on each side, some spruce boughs for carpet and I'd have a nice three-sided suite. It was much simpler to construct than a snow tunnel.

At last light, I was wrapped like a burrito, staring into the campfire, chewing on a piece of jerky. It was time to contemplate: I had departed the cave twenty-eight days ago. I estimated the distance traveled to be around 70 to 80 miles but my total "straight-line" progress to be only about half that amount due to circuitous meandering forced upon me by the geographical lay of the land.

There had also been weather delays and the time it had taken to re-construct the snowshoes and sled. The only way I had managed to get this far was by staying on the move every time I had moonlight. At this pace, it would take at least an additional twenty-four to twenty-eight days to reach the highway. That was far longer than I had anticipated.

Questions bombarded my mind: Should I risk traveling in colder weather? What about my food supply? Should I take the time to hunt and trap or just do a death march for the highway? Lastly, how many more fires could I make?

On the first question: The coldest I had ever seen it in Fairbanks was -68 degrees Fahrenheit. That cold spell had lasted three very long weeks. The extremely low temps we in the far north endure aren't so bad when they are short-lived. But the longer they last, the more stuff starts breaking down. Vehicles, furnaces, machinery, and people begin to fail under the strain of severe cold. I was really praying that another cold front would not move in, but if one did, that it wouldn't last long. But what if it did? How long could I endure severe cold? What was the absolute lowest temperature I could survive while hiking? I finally concluded, wise or unwise, that if I never took chances, if I always played it safe and never rose to the challenge, I might never make it home. As long as I could avoid the deadly threats of sweat, whiteouts, and leads, I was convinced I could travel and survive severely cold weather. Maybe not -68 degrees, but I felt confident that I could handle -40. If temps dropped lower than that and I was running out of food, I'd just have to take my chances and hit the frozen trail.

On the second question: I already knew I didn't have enough meat to last another three to four weeks. At best, if I carefully rationed the jerky, I had a two-week supply. I could also consume the bear and moose fat, but that would buy me only a couple of days' nutrition. I must kill or catch more food. Yet hunting and trapping could easily extend this ordeal indefinitely.

In addition, I had no means by which to kill a large animal. Though I had seen caribou, they had been scattered far and wide, no more than little dots in the distance. They have great eyesight and, because they are continually harassed by predators, are as difficult to approach as antelope on the wide-open prairie. Had I the ability to build a bow, complete with straight arrows, I might be able to get close enough to a moose or moose calf to kill it but I had no archery crafting skills and doubted I could make something with enough thrust to pierce their tough hide.

Snaring a small critter like a snowshoe hare or a red squirrel was possible but would force me to gamble precious time with a slim chance at success.

Ptarmigan were abundant but difficult enough to sneak up on with a shotgun, much less with just a rock or a stick.

Then there were grouse. Grouse were also abundant in the area. I had been seeing them every few days. Ruffed and spruce grouse were common across much of our state, including south of the Brooks. Spruce grouse were the dumb ones. If hunted properly, they would sit there until you were almost close enough to kick them. They were grossly over-confident in their camouflage.

My greatest chance, then, at getting extra protein was in grouse hunting. Every seasoned Alaskan hunter has at least one story of killing a spruce grouse with a rock or a stick. I have one friend who took his boot off in camp and killed a grouse with it. When he recounted the story, I teasingly suggested that the bird could've been killed just as easily by the odor from the boot as by blunt force trauma.

Were it not for the likelihood of killing a few spruce grouse, I might have been forced into a life or death marathon to the Dalton, almost nonstop. My chances of surviving such a taxing endeavor would be slight. So, if I were to avoid starvation, my best bet would be to watch carefully for wild chicken and to set one or two snares every night (or day) before retiring. I would then check them first thing before packing up and heading out. I must also initiate this plan immediately. Hopefully, I would have success before my supply of meager fare disappeared.

Regarding the final question: I had taken inventory before turning in for the night. Only three matches remained. I might be able to produce fire from just the sparks that emanated from the empty lighter, but I couldn't pin my hopes on it. One thing I had no experience in, sadly, was producing fire using primitive methods.

From now on, I must use fire only when my life depended on it and pray for the temps not to drop exceedingly. However, the likelihood of avoiding severe cold in the Arctic for three or more weeks was very slim. Of this I was acutely aware.

These were the stark realities that confronted me, and these were the resulting decisions I made that night on the trail. I clung to the hope that barring any unforeseen circumstances, I should still come out of this alive. However, it was those "unforeseen" things that were constantly nipping at the back of my mind.

The unknown haunted me. Fear followed me. Every time it did, however, I gave it to God.

"Lord, you spared my life on the mountain, you spared my life in the valley, and I believe you will do so again and again until I am safely home with my family. When that happens, and even now, I surrender to your perfect will for my life, whatever that may be. I belong to you. Please protect me from my own impatience, from foolish decisions, and from this ferocious, frozen wilderness."

Each time I prayed that prayer or one similar to it, great peace moved in, great worry moved out. As fearsome as this arctic wilderness was, my God, the God of the Bible, created it. He was greater than the Brooks Range. He was greater than all of creation. And He was mine. And I? Well, I was gladly His.

No power in heaven, on earth, or under the earth could touch me without His permission. And if He gave His permission, He would also give His grace.

"My grace is sufficient for you," God told the apostle Paul, "for my strength is made perfect in weakness" [2 Cor. 12:9]. If weakness was the condition for receiving God's grace, I must be the number one candidate, at least for now.

I felt very weak, very small, and very helpless immersed in this beautiful but deadly land. But God was teaching me and molding me through this experience. I was learning that the smaller we realize we are, the more we depend upon God. And this, after all, is His delight.

Utter dependence upon God is actually a form of worship, of humbling one's self before Him. I needed humbling. No one but God knew that better than I.

Before this divinely appointed crisis, I had viewed myself as quite independent and strong, even smarter than most. How foolish. Over the past few months, I'd seen my true stature reflected in the face of death, reflected in dire need, and reflected by my fears; and I was ashamed—not of being afraid, but of my pride, of the exalted but warped picture I had painted of myself that no one saw but me. I was, until this God-ordained experience, "a legend in my own mind," as they say.

Well, no more. Through this experience, God had revealed a painful but accurate image of me—and it wasn't pretty.

Surely, this must be how the Old Testament prophet Isaiah felt when he saw God "high and lifted up," and cried:

"Woe is me! For I am undone [coming apart]! because I am a man of unclean lips, and I dwell in the midst of a people of unclean lips; for my eyes have seen the King, the LORD of hosts" [Isa. 6:1, 5].

Though I haven't, like Isaiah, seen God with my physical eyes, I have seen God in His Word, in His creation, in my faith, and in life's valleys.

At the same time, I have seen myself, and I don't like what I have seen: a deceitful, proud, self-absorbed man. I felt convicted, bothered, and saddened by my reflection, by the reality of who and what I was.

Quite suddenly, though, the remedy came to me.

I knelt in the snow and confessed my sinful condition in the presence of a Holy God and cried for forgiveness, all the while thanking Him for His mercy, grace, love, and longsuffering for truly, He is a great and terrible God, yet one who has been appeased once and for all by the atoning work of His beloved Son, the Lord Jesus Christ.

"He shall see the labor of His soul, and shall be satisfied" [Isa. 53:11].

I began to tearfully praise His name: "Thank God the Father for God the Son and God the Holy Spirit, the Great Three-in-One! The true and living triune God is eternal, personal, perfect, and loving. He knows all things and is in control even when it appears to finite beings like us that the world is one big ball of mass confusion. It isn't.

Everything is unfolding according to His will. And He, the Almighty, is tender and forgiving to those who are of a contrite heart.

"For thus says the High and Lofty One who inhabits eternity, whose name is Holy; 'I dwell in the high and holy place, with him who has a contrite and humble spirit" [Isa. 57:15].

And, "a broken and a contrite heart—These, O God, You will not despise" [Ps. 51:17].

God the Father planned our creation and redemption, God the Son provided for it by offering His own self as a sacrifice for our sins, and God the Holy Spirit presided over it, ensuring its fulfillment.

The same eternal Three-in-One brought the world and all that is into existence-

The Father planned it, Christ commanded it to appear, and the

Spirit "was hovering over the face of the waters" [Genesis 1]. It is no wonder that the Lord Jesus is called *the Word* in Scripture [John 1: 1-3; Rev. 19:13]. After all, it was He, amongst the Godhead, who spoke… and it appeared! [Col. 1: 13-19]

By the time I was done, my spirit had been renewed.

As I brushed the snow off my knees and trudged along, these wonderful truths flooded my soul, truths I had learned years ago directly from the Holy Bible in Genesis chapter 1, John chapter 1, Ephesians chapter 1, Colossians chapter 1, Hebrews chapter 1, and Revelation chapter 1.

I recalled that when all of these "first chapters" in Scripture are combined, compared, and believed, the honest, seeking soul will come to certain, absolute conclusions:

God is three persons in perfect unity—the Great Three-in One. He created all things; He knew ahead of time that man would fall away from Him by choosing to sin; He provided for our salvation in His eternal Son, Jesus Christ; and He designed the entire plan "before the foundation of the world" [Ephesians 1:4; 1 Peter 1:18-20; Revelation 13:8].

And the purpose of it all is to bring glory to Himself throughout eternity.

For sinful man to desire, to scheme, to crave glory or praise as I had done is vain because we, as sinful humans, do not deserve such praise. But the God of all creation both *deserves* all glory, all honor, and all praise and *demands* it… and *will* receive it throughout eternity according to His perfect plan [Revelation chapter 5].

Recalling all of this made me feel very small, yet very significant; undeserving, yet grateful to God beyond measure for His mercy and grace bestowed upon me, his fallen creature.

Meditating upon the greatness of God and His awesome love for me was the perfect way to pass the time over the next few days as I navigated through deep snow, hobbled over frozen tundra, and warily crossed frozen rivers, sloughs, and lakes.

Slowly, the miles piled up behind me.

Each day brought with it a mix of good things and bad—more sunlight yet more cold, more progress but less food.

All I could do was take it one day and one step at a time. And on nights when I was too anxious to relax, I prayed until my eyes grew heavy, and eventually, fell asleep.

"Day thirty-four on the trail," I said, while tying the sled harness around my waist.

I had not used fire in quite a while. My match count was still three, but my plastic lighter was finally spent.

Fortunately, the weather had been tolerable. Only twice had I been forced to dig a snow cave and light the lamp for heat. I had tried to carry fire with me in the form of smoldering cottonwood but to no avail. It lasted a few hours and died out in spite of the CPR I gave it.

I looked skyward, squinting in the late morning sun. The high clouds were moving out. I guess I'd better move out as well.

That night I set up camp under the stars, next to a wide drainage. It was colder, but the winds were calm. I would light no fire tonight.

Even though my sleeping bag wasn't rated for these extreme conditions and was beginning to show serious signs of wear and tear, I still had the tarp, an unlimited supply of spruce boughs, and the bear hide. Those items, along with my hunting jacket, warm hat, gloves, and long johns, provided enough insulation. I was more comfortable than I had anticipated.

To insure that there was absolutely no moisture in my underwear and long underwear when sleeping, I removed the underclothes I had been hiking in through the day (or night), placed them in the bottom of my sleeping bag along with my socks. My own body heat acted as a clothes dryer during the night. Upon waking, I found that any item of clothing that had spent the night in my bag was bone dry. With two pairs of everything, I could alternate the pairs. That way the clothing next to my skin stayed completely dry, at least when I was not moving.

My preparation for sleep was as follows: First, I'd place spruce boughs on snow-covered ground. Since snow acts as an insulator, it is warmer to lie on than bare, frozen ground. Then, while standing on the tarp, I'd remove my boots, pants, jacket, outer shirt, long johns, t-shirt, and underwear. Very quickly, I put on the under-clothes and long johns that had dried the night before. Next, the boots went back on my feet, temporarily allowing me to fold the tarp several times and place it on top of a thick bed of boughs. Then I removed the boots, crawled into the bag, rolled up my jacket for a pillow, and pulled the bear hide over my entire curled up body, face and all. Lastly, I pulled my wool hat as far over my face as it would go and placed the quilted shirt around my neck and shoulders. Not one item was wasted.

The use of every item of clothing to stay warm reminded me of a hunting trip years ago when I forgot my sleeping bag. Unfortunately, it was late in the fall season and in a low area (Minto Flats), which made it colder at night. I had provided sleeping gear for two friends and my son, but in the process, I had forgotten my own. My brother-in-law, Jim, loaned me his army poncho liner. That's all I had to keep warm at night other than the clothes I was wearing and one change of everything. I didn't even have an air mat. In spite of my mistake and in spite of the temperature dropping to fifteen or twenty degrees Fahrenheit at night, I stayed relatively warm, albeit, not exactly cozy.

I found this method I used years ago to be very helpful in this present ordeal and whenever I got caught by severe cold, I stopped an hour early, dug a snow cave and enacted the above-mentioned process as best I could.

Regardless, on those forty-below nights I was not comfortable, but neither was I in danger of freezing to death. To survive extremely low temps required every ounce of creativity, every item in my supply, and every bit of knowledge gleaned from the past. The dry clothes, the bag, the hat, the hide, the spruce boughs, the tarp, the snow cave, and the candle, all combined, barely protected me from the frozen fingers of death.

On day thirty-six, about two hours before light, I arose, ready to march.

I dearly wanted a mug of hot Chaga before hitting the trail but drank it cold instead. For breakfast, I ate a piece of frozen moose jerky and then solemnly gathered my gear. All that remained in my food stash was a few small pieces of meat and a little moose fat.

I must've jinxed myself by determining to kill grouse and set snares. I hadn't seen one game bird since that time and though I had set probably twenty snares over the past week and a half, the score was critters—20; me—0.

As I departed the campsite, I figured out that since leaving the bear cave I'd built over two dozen shelters. Some had been as simple as a modified deadfall or standing spruce overhang. Others had been more elaborate, such as snow caves or willow huts covered with spruce boughs. Several nights I had slept where I fell, too tired to care about such luxuries.

In any case, I was making progress. Things were encouraging on the one hand, discouraging on the other. So I determined to think only upon the encouraging hand and, as I had many times before, set my face eastward.

— 16 —
THE CONFUSION

Surprisingly, the miles behind me were really adding up. Over a month of hiking through this harsh land had me in top shape. I guessed my weight to be around 165 pounds, down from my normal of 185 pounds. I had cut two more holes in my belt just to get it tight enough around my waist. My upper body was only slightly stronger than normal, but my lower body and leg muscles were rock hard.

Taking the journey one step, one hour, and one mile at a time, I pressed on. Sometimes I sang, sometimes I prayed, but most of the time, I just listened to my own huffing and puffing: inhale once, exhale twice; inhale twice, exhale once. This was my silent mantra, hours at a time. I stopped only to relieve myself, eat a swab of fat, and rehydrate.

My meat supply was almost depleted. I had prepared and filled my pack with meat before departure but now had just three pieces of jerky and some fat in a small plastic baggie. If I could just figure out this food shortage, I could be home with my family in less than a month. That one thought spurred me on.

That night, while kneeling over my pack, I began to think aloud:

"The fat will provide some nutrition. If I ration the jerky at one stick per day and eat the animal fat, I still will have only a few days of meager sustenance."

In reality, I'd need far more calories than a piece of jerky and a smidgen of fat each day to sustain the kind of physical exertion this journey required.

The berries were long gone. The Chaga along with spruce needles might very well be a lifesaver for me if I couldn't snare a rabbit or kill some grouse or ptarmigan. Surely, I could at least find some forest fowl. Alaska was ripe with upland game birds year around. All were delectable except the spruce grouse. They could be a little gamey, as they tasted a lot like liver. However, since I like liver and since I was currently in no position to be picky, even a spruce grouse would be a treat. Right then, I determined to double the intensity of my protein search and be on the lookout for any extra food source. I must harvest something with which to supplement my diet, or very soon I'd be in trouble.

Contemplating my dilemma, I packed up and continued hiking. I no longer allowed myself to daydream. Instead, I scoured every tree, every willow, and every snowy mound for potential meals. I had at least another fifty to sixty miles before I reached the Dalton Highway.

Since my journey had taken almost forty days to reach this point, I knew it would take at least another twenty days to completion, depending on the weather.

I continued to search and pray earnestly for protein. It wasn't until halfway through the next day that I spotted movement near some spruce trees—it was a grouse!

Immediately I dropped my pack and scoured the area for more birds since they tend to stay together. I counted three. They were moving in and out from under the trees, pecking the bare ground in search of tiny pieces of grit. Clinging to the hope that these birds were as dumb as others I had encountered over the years, I crept closer. Fortunately, these had probably never seen a human. I scoured the snow-covered ground looking for a bump that might indicate a rock or a stick. Luckily, I found and quickly grabbed a nice billy-club-sized diamond willow.

Immediately, their heads shot straight up like little antennae. They froze, and so did I.

Just ten more yards, and I could attempt to stun one by throwing the cave-man weapon. Suddenly, they flushed… gone!

"Gone!" I shouted, as they flew at the horizon.

I spat and and fumed and pouted and kicked the snow and tried not to say bad words. Even though these birds hadn't been hunted by man and should've been easy prey, they spooked. And I immediately recalled why:

The biggest problem I face when wing-shooting spruce grouse is getting them to fly. Since I don't own a bird dog, I quickly learned the best way to get the dumb birds to flush is to imitate a predator like a fox or a lynx. If you walk towards them quickly, steadily, standing tall, they ignore you, and you can just about kick them. But if you start creeping up on them like a predator, the way I just foolishly had, they fly.

Now that's perfect if you're shot-gunning, but not if you're a desperate, soon-to-be-starving idiot such as I. Of course, by the time I remembered this tiny but important piece of information, they were in flight, zipping through the trees like miniature fighter jets.

"Oh well," I muttered in disgust, "Next time, I'll march right at 'em and grab 'em with my bare hands!"

Two more days passed, and I was down to eating the last of the fat. Wow. What a breakfast.

Within minutes of leaving camp, though, I had another chance at some grouse. These were ruffed grouse, and they were bunched together in a tall willow bush, eating the buds. It was loaded with about half a dozen birds.

I had encountered this scene one other time while on a fall moose hunt several years earlier. My buddy Neal and I had a .22 with us. We spotted eight or ten birds, right at dusk, eating the buds off a willow bush. After finding a good rest, we took turns picking them off until we had as many as we wanted. We strategically chose the one nearest the bottom of the bush and shot it first, then the next one up, and so on, so as not to spook them all. Had we shot the highest bird first, it would've fallen into the rest, flapping its wings and making a ruckus. The others would've flown. Our plan worked perfectly, and we ended up with four ruffed grouse breasts for dinner that night. Now that was one tasty meal!

Ruffed grouse are much more desirable than spruce grouse. Their meat is white and very mild on the pallet because they don't eat spruce needles like their counterpart. Instead, their diet consists of berries and willow buds. However, ruffed and sharp-tailed grouse are also more difficult to bag because they are smarter, at least when they're on the ground. In other words, when alarmed, they run like pheasants. If the hunter is committed to wing-shooting them but doesn't have a dog, he will rarely get a shot.

Luckily for me, these ruffed grouse weren't on the ground. They were in an oversized willow bush and felt safe, so they just ignored me.

I knew exactly what to do: lumber right under them like a lazy moose and then, WHACK!

I did so and… it worked! I clobbered one with my walking stick. With a great noise, they all flew away with the exception of one. He flapped his wings something fierce but to no avail. I pounced on it like a half-starved Lynx!

"Nice!" I exclaimed with glee. I held in my hand a beautiful, fat, juicy bird for the fire tonight. It was a fortunate kill because I had just one spoonful of fat left, and it wasn't even bear fat.

Normally, upon harvesting a grouse, I simply remove the breast and toss the rest. There is very little meat anywhere else on the bird. However, every morsel was vital to me in this situation. In camp that night, I painstakingly plucked the bird. Every ounce of meat would be consumed, including the heart, liver, gizzard, and other organs. The feathers I used to line my gloves. That one small addition really made a difference in keeping my hands warm.

Over the next three days, I spotted grouse regularly. But seeing them didn't always translate into roasting them over the fire. I threw sticks, rocks, and even snowballs at them. One day I attempted a stalk, got very close, and then tried to pounce on them, but to no avail. After half a dozen failed attempts, I managed to bag only one more bird. It was a spruce grouse that, as expected, tasted like liver. But the gamey flavor didn't bother me in the least.

My mind continually wandered to food. The next day, I settled for cold soup using the internal organs of the bird, some Rosehips, and a spruce twig. I was hungry enough that it was quite enjoyable, and it gave me a much-needed shot of energy. By nightfall, I was not as hungry as I was weak. I could tell my body was really burning the calories. The rigors of the journey and the cold were taking their toll. I cut two more holes in my belt and knew my days were numbered if I couldn't find sustenance.

I prayed. I contemplated. I schemed and I dreamed…of food.

I set snares on fresh rabbit tracks and waited, watching at a distance for an entire day. If a watched pot never boils, a watched snare surely never catches. I spent a lot of time and effort for nothing.

I painstakingly gathered a handful of frozen, shriveled rosehips at every opportunity. They were sparse, but a few stubbornly clung to the bushes in areas protected from wind. Though they were very rich in vitamin C, I needed more than rosehips to survive.

I was losing more weight. The griz poncho swallowed me up like a bedspread. One day, upon removing my glove, my wedding band fell off. Thankfully, I found it and placed it in my pocket. Even my boots felt loose, so I had to tighten the laces. The drastic weight loss frightened me.

Night came quickly but not as quickly as it had a week earlier. I estimated that it was nearing the end of January. Daylight had been increasing, very slowly, since December 22. I recalled that at one time I thought I might actually make it home for Christmas. Now I knew I'd be blessed to make it home alive.

The sky was clear and the stars were brilliant, but it was definitely getting colder. I didn't have the strength to dig a snow cave. I did, however, make camp under the branches of a giant standing spruce. I remember that particular tree. It was quite impressive.

With the ice-cold breath of death on the back of my neck, I gathered tinder, sticks, and as much wood as I could find and carefully prepared to light what would probably be my last fire. I had just one more match for one more fire. I knew I'd probably have only one chance to light the birch bark, so I had to make sure everything was ready. One strike . . . one flame . . . one chance.

As I built the nest of tender, I recalled Jack London's short story "To Build a Fire." It goes something like this: A man and his dog team were caught in the wilderness during a whiteout. Then the weather turned bitterly cold, like -45 or something crazy like that. He tried to start a fire and failed several times till he was down to one match. So he got everything perfectly ready underneath a big spruce tree; the sled dogs were curled up all around him, their noses tucked inside their warm fur.

Then he lit his very last match and got a wonderful, roaring bonfire going. Just as he and his dogs were getting warm, there was a dreadful crash, and a gigantic load of snow from above fell on him, his dogs, and, worst of all, his fire. He was found weeks later, frozen solid, under that spruce tree. He had made the tragic mistake of starting his fire under a tree whose branches were loaded with snow. Once the heat from the fire warmed up the man, his dogs, and, unfortunately, the branches, the snow gave way and came crashing down.

When I first read that story as a kid, I thought the dramatic surprise ending was great. But now it seemed too close to reality to be considered entertainment. With the unfortunate frozen dude in mind, I knocked the snow off the branches above my lair before striking the match.

"Scratch!" The tiny flame exploded at the end of the little stick. My hands were shaking, due partly to the cold and partly to nerves. The paper birch bark accepted the flame readily as it always does. The tinder caught fire. As meticulously as an engineer, I added small sticks to the flame and then larger ones. Soon I had a mug of hot water and rosehips. That was my supper. It warmed me considerably, but I knew the little bit of energy it gave would be short lived, as would I, if I couldn't find food.

Not knowing how long this cold spell would last, I really needed to gather a ton of firewood, but my strength was gone. I ventured out forty to fifty yards, picked up a few chunks in the moonlight, returned to my crude shelter, and collapsed. Each time the fire dwindled down to coals, I was forced to repeat the routine. And each time, I became weaker and colder.

Then, it happened. I slept too long. Startled, I jumped out from under the bear rug. It was too late. The fire had burned all its fuel and gone out long before. The ashes were cold… and so was I.

I got up, searched every corner of my pack for a match, a morsel—anything that would help me through the night. I found nothing but a few chunks of Chaga. I put some of the shavings from the pumice in my mouth, hoping to draw some strength from it. It actually did revive me a little. I ate some snow even though I knew that doing so is a tradeoff. Eating snow hydrates but also burns calories and lowers one's body temp. Oh well. I was too weak to care. I was discouraged, half frozen, and physically drained. Yet I desired to live. I lay there quite a while, too scared to fall asleep. I might not live through this one.

Eventually, I got up, filled my plastic water bag with snow, added some Chaga and Rosehips, sealed it tightly, and put it inside the sleeping bag so that the snow would melt. At least it would provide something of an energy drink in the morning. Upon further contemplation, I added spruce needles and a couple of rosehips. It was two notches below meager but one notch above starvation.

Late into the next morning, with just a hint of morning glow on the horizon, I once again set my frozen face toward civilization. I was dangerously weak and found it difficult to concentrate. The snowshoes had been left behind. I just didn't have the strength required to use them. About forty to fifty miles remained in this journey—or was it further? Where were the mountains, the big ones? Was this the right direction? Was I lost?

There, to my left was one of the peaks of the Brooks! Though I was stumbling more than walking, at least I was stumbling toward the road. It seemed worlds away, but I encouraged myself in two ways:

(1) I compared the remaining distance to how far I'd come.

(2) I prayed.

I didn't have the energy to pray out loud. But I knew the Spirit of God was within and would intercede for me. In my unspoken prayers, I reasoned with God as I had many times before:

"Lord God of all creation, You have brought me this far—surely, not to die. I am finite. You are infinite. I am mortal. You are eternal. You know all things. I know nothing. If indeed there is a purpose to all of this—this journey—please help me escape the Brooks, return to my family, and live out that purpose."

Silently, I prayed this prayer and many similar to it.

My progress was worse than slow. I had to rest frequently because of fatigue. However, I was in a "catch 22" situation. Each time I stopped to rest, I'd become extremely cold, mentally foggy, and physically incapacitated. I could not rest more than two to three minutes at a time. Nevertheless, I hobbled on. One mile; then two, or was it really just one? I did not know nor did I care. In that moment, I lost heart. My will to survive, to live, to anything, imploded.

With the last ounce of energy given me by chewing on a piece of Chaga, I dug a shallow snow cave and crawled in, fully dressed. The sun was still shining.

"Who cares?" My mind spoke but my mouth did not.

I should continue on...but I was done.

"This is where I will die," I whispered and fell into a deep sleep.

I dreamed profusely. I had dreams about forest fires, chimney fires, campfires. I even dreamed of hell, of smoke . . . of warmth . . . of heat. Then I was rescuing someone from a house fire—

Suddenly, I awoke, screaming and slapping my legs. I thought they were on fire. I lay back on the tarp, heart pounding, shivering. I was surprised...and somewhat disappointed to be alive.

I closed my frosted eyelids and tried to escape reality.

It was at that moment I was jolted by a bolt of lightning! It jarred me to the marrow of my bones and sat me straight up so fast that I hit my head on the top of the snow cave.

"OUCH!" I shouted. Instantly, adrenaline shot through my body from my wool hat all the way down to my worn out boots.

"Do I smell smoke?! Wood smoke!?"

Hurriedly, I rolled onto my stomach and tried crawling backwards out of the cave but got tangled up in the griz poncho. Kicking, grunting, groaning, spinning, straining, shuffling . . . it seemed like forever and a day, but finally, I was outside.

I stood to my feet. I could feel the blood pulsating in my neck. Am I dreaming? I thought I smelled wood smoke and . . .

"NO, I AIN'T DREAMIN!" I shouted the answer to my doubting soul.

It was as real as the ice on my beard. I smelled wood smoke and wood smoke meant humans. It was highly unlikely that there would be a forest fire this time of year. Sometimes forest fires can actually smolder underground through the entire winter, but that occurrence is rare. Besides, this didn't smell like smoldering tundra. This smelled like birch, like spruce...

"IT SMELLS LIKE HOME!!"

There was no doubt in my mind. It had to be smoke from a woodstove or campfire. Is that why I dreamed of fire all night long? Someone had to be in a camp or cabin nearby.

"I SMELL FREEDOM!" I proclaimed, once again, to the top of my frozen voice.

— 17 —
THE CABIN

At once, I was a basket case of mixed emotions. I was excited, surprised, nervous, thrilled—and very scared. It was difficult to absorb such an array of feelings all at once. I began to shiver, but not from the cold. I grabbed my pack, tried to collect my belongings as well as my thoughts and began to walk in a large circle like I did when tracking an animal. Except this time, I wasn't looking for tracks or a blood trail. This time, I was sniffing, taking in the air, gently.

"Stay calm," I coached myself. "Sniff slowly and lightly or you might lose the scent."

Suddenly: "There it is! I've got it!"

Once I had the direction, I started walking into the breeze and thereby the smell. It was the joyful odor of rescue . . . of escape . . . of life. It wasn't long before I could actually see the wisp of gray smoke suspended like a ghostly snake. The more I followed it, the easier it became to see. It was gunpowder gray, about head high. The sight now led me as much as the distinct, comforting aroma. They say our sense of smell triggers our memory like none of the other senses. I believed it. The joy of possibly being rescued at such a crucial time was tempered only by the fond memories of house and home, generated by the wonderful smell.

Cautiously, afraid of losing the floating trail, I crept closer to the source. I had just crested a wooded hill when, suddenly, a cabin came into view. It was picturesque: a small, spruce log structure set in the white snow, framed by the beauty of the Arctic sky. It reminded me of a Machetanz painting.[16] I stood there in awe of the scene, the colors, and the thought of being rescued. I suppose I was

---

[16] Fred Machetanz was one of the most prolific Alaskan artists in modern times. One of his specialties was capturing the unique colors of mid-winter in the arctic.

paralyzed by joy.

As cold and hungry and weak as I was, I knelt to offer thanks to God, the God of all that is. This was an epic moment in my life and I knew it.

I knelt there and prayed until a tear trickled halfway down my face and froze. That got my attention. I arose and moved forward. However, as soon as I took that first step towards the cabin, fear and doubt came upon me. Would the occupants be friendly or angry? Lawful and peaceful, or lawless and violent? Any of these were possible this far from civilization. Alaska is literally "the end of the road" for a lot of people. Many come to the far north running from the law, family, reality, or all the above. I was nervous. But I was also desperate. The only strength I had left was from the raw adrenaline that coursed through my emaciated body. I had no food and nothing with which to start a fire. I was afraid but was also more than willing to take my chances with whatever or whoever was on the other side of that cabin door. I wasn't about to let my fearful imagination steal what could very well be my one opportunity for freedom. It was do or die.

With this mindset, I took another step and then another. Every split second of every detail of these few moments in time is permanently carved in my memory. I started walking slowly and methodically toward the porch. Twelve steps.

Soon, I came upon two sets of fresh snow-machine tracks. Was it two machines or one machine coming and going? I needed as much information as possible before taking the risk of knocking on that door.

However, I also needed food, water, and warmth. Five more steps and I was on the porch. I walked up to the door and knocked timidly. Nothing. I knocked louder, waited, and then pounded several times. Still nothing. I walked around the cabin. "Hello?" I called, voice trembling.

This must be someone's trap-line cabin. They're out checking traps while it's daylight. If I was correct, that'd be a good sign, because anyone who runs a trap line has to have a good work ethic and most criminals are lazy.

It didn't take long for me to confirm my theory. There was a small shed around back, full of trapping supplies. This encouraged me greatly, so I walked back around and up the cabin steps. Very slowly, I turned the knob and opened the door. "HELLO? ANYBODY HERE?" Except for the occasional popping of spruce in the woodstove, all was silent.

Obviously, no one was around. Even so, I crept silently inside and closed the door. The cabin was warm. I could feel the comforting balm of woodstove heat being absorbed by my cold bones. It felt as good as the hot springs!

I just stood there soaking it up while evaluating my surroundings. I was trying to learn as much about the occupants as possible before they returned. I was extremely nervous. This was trespassing, but I prayed the owner would forgive me this once. Suddenly I realized I was standing on a mat that read "WELCOME." This made me smile. "I hope you mean it," I thought aloud.

The floor plan was very simple: one room, sixteen by twenty feet. The kitchen was to my right, a set of bunks to my left, and the woodstove against the back wall, dead center, with a coffee pot on the flat top. I must've stared at that pot in pleasant shock for at least a full minute and wondered if it held any black gold.

Over on the kitchen side was a card table. On that table I spotted what appeared to be a pint jar of smoked salmon and a box of Sailor Boy Crackers. My mouth began to water. I could not resist. I walked over, opened the jar, and placed a piece of salmon on the edge of one of the saucer-sized crackers. Then I took a giant bite as big as a northern pike eatin' a duck. Saliva filled my mouth. The fish was indescribably good, and not just because I was half-starved. It was smoky, salty, spicy, and slightly sweet, all at once. It was moist, not overcooked like a lot of smoked salmon. These guys knew how to treat their fish! Immediately, my body absorbed the nutrition like the desert absorbs rain. It was beyond glorious.

I had not forgotten the coffee. No way. My own mama would forget my name before I'd forget that pot of heavenly nectar. Having been on the stove all day, it was as thick and black as used oil. It was rotgut and absolutely wonderful!

Without remorse, I sat down at the little table, polished off the fish, most of the crackers, and every drop of the wicked java.

About an hour of daylight remained outside, but inside it was already dark. I looked out the window just above where I had been sitting. I neither saw nor heard anything, so I lit the lantern hanging over the table and brewed a fresh pot. When it percolated, I thought I heard the angels in heaven singing. It brought to mind Raymond Chandler's words in *The Long Goodbye*:

"I went out to the kitchen to make coffee. Rich, strong, bitter, boiling, hot, ruthless, depraved. The life blood of tired men."

Normally I don't drink this much coffee in one sitting, but I knew I'd probably fall asleep in the chair if I didn't. That's the best excuse I could come up with, and since I'd need to be wide-awake if the trapper returned, I felt it was a good one.

My musings were brought to a sudden halt by the roar of a snow machine. The noise revived my conscience. Guilt and fear interrupted the peaceful setting. The short-lived party was over. I stood up from the table about the time the door opened. It swung open very slowly, hinges squeaking. For one moment, all I could see was wood. Then I saw the shotgun barrel.

It was the moment of truth, of fear, and of borderline panic.

A native man stepped forward, turned and faced me. As unhappy as this moment was, I could not help but notice that he was wearing the most beautiful beaver-pelt parka I've ever seen. The hood was trimmed in wolverine. His mukluks looked to be made of sealskin and caribou. He had on military issue wool pants. As much as I was impressed by his appearance, he appeared shocked by mine. His jaw dropped.

Very quickly, I became awfully self-conscious. For months, I had only been seen by ravens, caribou, moose, wolverine and a giant griz. Now, however, I was being stared at by another human.

There I stood, trembling, skinny as a starved dog, the bear hide dwarfing my frail frame and my face covered in almost five months of growth. I held my wool hat in my hand, turning it nervously. My blue jeans were torn, with long johns exposed; my leather boots had wolverine fur hanging out the tops. I hadn't felt embarrassed in a long time, but I did now, and even more so upon realizing that I was holding his coffee cup.

"Oops," I half whispered. In my world, and I'm sure his, a man's coffee mug is sacred.

He was an Eskimo about forty-something years of age. Although he didn't point the gun at me, he looked like he wanted to. I could tell he wasn't happy. He was tense, ready for anything.

Suddenly, from behind him stepped a boy about ten years of age. He was dressed similarly and held a .22 rifle in one hand, two white ptarmigan in the other. He wore a trapper's hat made of silver fox. It was pitch black, as were his eyes. Had I not been so scared, this would've been an impressive scene, one worth painting. In this moment, though, fear and trepidation outweighed awe.

The man spoke firmly, in short, cut-off words:

"This my mother's allotment."

I knew immediately what he meant. His mother had been given this parcel of land as a result of the Alaska Native Claims Settlement Act of 1971. At that time, the federal government gave Alaska natives millions of acres of land, recognizing their rights as the first residents of Alaska. The act was controversial to put it mildly, but the fact remained that it was the law.

And right now, I was on the wrong side of the law. So, basically, this man with a 12-gauge shotgun halfway pointed at me, was informing me in the briefest way possible that I was not just a trespasser but a really wicked, offensive one. I was standing on his family inheritance, given to his people by the U. S. government. I'm sure it didn't help that I was holding his coffee mug.

"Nothing like adding fuel to the fire," I thought, in self-rebuke.

At his declaration of my transgression, and fully comprehending all the condemnation that was packed in his one, short sentence, the hundred and one emotions that had been bottled up inside me for the past fist-full of months got the best of me. All of my new-found strength instantly vaporized, and my legs gave way.

I sat down hard, buried my head in my arms and wept. I cried loudly, very loudly. I completely lost control of myself for the second time on this journey. Only this time, I was ashamed. I was in the company of humans. I wanted very badly to explain what I'd been through or at the very least to declare that I'm not weak, I'm not wicked, I'm not a criminal nor a thief, but that I was, I was . . .

…helpless, very hungry, cold, and, yes…very sorry!

I tried to talk but all I could do was sob. My weeping literally turned to wailing. I did not even recognize the noise coming from my throat as belonging to me. Every crisis, every close call and every catastrophe I had been through on this journey cascaded through me in that moment:

the loss of my best friend, the close encounters with death, the grueling conditions, the intense weakness, the confusion, the questions, the depression, the fears—all of it fell upon me in that moment of time.

My sudden outburst must've scared the poor man.

He leaned the gun against the wall and hurried to my side. He knelt beside me and awkwardly but gently tried to comfort me. He asked lots of questions, but it was at least fifteen minutes before I could speak; even then, my story was frequently interrupted by more emotional outbursts. By the time I got it all out and had told the story in broken sentences, he stepped back as if he was seeing a ghost. And maybe he was.

As I wiped away the tears and tried to get myself together again, he stood there, shaking his head and saying, "What a man! What a story!"

Once I finally got my face cleaned up, however, I replied, with as strong a voice as I could muster:

"No sir, it isn't 'what a man'; it's 'what a God'! The God of all creation rescued me from off that mountain, strengthened me against that bear, protected me from the cold, and provided for me every step of the way. He it is that brought me from death's door to your door. I must give Him all the glory."

Suddenly, I found new strength, took a deep breath, and loudly proclaimed:

"Were it not for the one true and living God, the God of the Bible, I'd be bear scat!"

There was a long, tense silence.

Then he grinned real big, stuck out his hand, and said,

"O.K., well, anyway . . . my name's Sonny."

Still trembling from head to toe, I stood as tall as I could:

"My name is Bruce."

We shook hands.

I was so relieved that I almost fainted, and I sat down hard again. As before, the chair was there to catch me.

— 18 —
THE COINCIDENCE

Not until then did I remember the boy. He had moved as far away from me as he could and was sitting on the bunk bed, eyes wide open. His demeanor was gentle. Something about him, though he hadn't said one word, was mysteriously familiar. There was a look of curiosity but also of compassion in his eyes.

"I'm sorry I ate your fish and most of your crackers, Sonny. I haven't eaten real food in several days."

"It's O.K., even though that was my last jar of smoked reds," he said teasingly.

Right away, I knew I was gonna like this guy. His sense of humor was a little dry and similar to mine.

"We don't get red salmon in Anaktuvuk, but my cousin lives in Fairbanks. We trade sometimes. He gives us smoked, canned reds, and we give him blueberry jam or bear fat. Don't worry, once he hears how my last pint of salmon got eaten, he'll send me a bunch more just for the story!"

At this, Sonny laughed heartily. Even the silent boy smiled. I ventured a question his way. "What's your name?" I asked. He just looked at his dad and then down at his hands.

"His name's Daniel," Sonny said. "He's my son and a good one. I couldn't run the trap line without him. He don't say much 'cause he's been through a lot lately but he's a really good kid."

Quietly, I wondered what this boy could've been through that had caused him so much inner pain. It's just my nature to want to help people who are hurting because I've been there myself. However, I was also very familiar with the native ways and how they don't open up to anybody unless they trust you. Not wanting to embarrass Daniel, I quickly changed the subject.

"So, you guys are from Anaktuvuk? That's quite a ways from here, isn't it?"

"Yes," Sonny said, but there's a traditional trail we use along the John River. It's not a bad trip if the snow is good and no storms come up real sudden."

"How far is it?"

"Oh, 'bout seventy-five miles north as the raven flies…takes two to three days depending on trail conditions. We have an emergency cabin at the halfway point on Wolverine Creek, but sometimes we get in a whiteout and have to dig a snow cave or build an igloo shelter. Most times though, we watch the forecast and wait for a decent report. Then we hop on the snow-go and harvest fur and either reset or pull traps as quickly as possible before bad weather arrives. This cabin is our turnaround point."

"Your village is a lot closer to where our plane crashed than the Dalton Highway," I said, "but I wasn't quite sure what direction it was. Besides, there's no way I could've crossed those intimidating mountains. Even though the Dalton was further, it was also easier to locate since all I had to do was follow a big river south until clear of the mountains; then I turned east and I knew that, eventually, I'd run into the road."

It was quiet for a while then I spoke again.

"So, you gotta trap line around here?"

"Yep," he replied, "we trap the John River from Anaktuvuk, south—all the way to our cabin here at Timber Creek."

"Is that where we are right now?" I asked.

"Yes, we're right now near Timber Creek at the base of Nine Mile Hills."

Then Sonny turned the tables on me.

"Why do you guys hunt so far from home? Isn't that a lot more expensive?" he asked.

"Well, for one thing, this country is addictive. I've been hunting and fishing around the Brooks for twenty-plus years. The main reason, though, is regulations."

"Regulations?" he queried.

"Yes, the regulations have become so restrictive and our old stompin' grounds so overrun with hunters from Anchorage and the Kenai that we started huntin' up here just to escape the pressure."

"So, where do you guys hunt, and how far from here did your

plane crash?"

We've hunted the Colville and Chandler Rivers, north of the range, but this time we thought we'd try the Killik River. As we were attempting to get through the pass, the weather turned so bad so quickly that we couldn't see a thing. It was as though someone plastered the windshield with white paper. We tried climbing out of it, and, well, the rest you already know."

"How far away from here did you crash?"

''I hiked, lunged, and zigzagged for probably 120 miles or so before finding your cabin, but I would guess the crash site to be no more than 70-80 miles northwest of here in a straight line. We tried to land on a boulder-strewn flat spot in the mountains. It was our only hope. I survived the crash landing…my buddy did not." For a moment, there was an uncomfortable silence then, I continued:

"Once I descended the plateau, I found the cave and holed up there for three months waiting on freeze-up. Then, I followed a major drainage downstream about twenty-five miles, turned east, meandered about one hundred miles, and here I am."

"Sounds like you were near the Arrigetch Mountains," he said. "Were they really rugged looking, like, more than usual?"

"Oh yes," I responded. "They were jagged, fearsome and… well, awesome, all at once. A few of them looked like natural cathedral spires"

"Yep, that's the Arrigetch Mountains, and that big river you followed was the Alatna. Man, you're really lucky if you crashed and survived anywhere in that country. That's some of the most deadly terrain in the world."

"Well, I believe God spared my life for a reason. I'm just not quite sure why yet."

Sonny ignored my God-comment, so I changed the subject.

"Hey Sonny, are you guys familiar with a natural hot springs near those mountains?"

"Actually, there are several of them in the Brooks, but only two that our people use and have used for centuries. Why? Did you find one?" He asked, grinning.

"Yes!" I responded with enthusiasm.

"As I was following a little creek the day after descending the mountain, I stumbled upon a hot springs. It had a very old-looking stone wall around it. I rested and soaked there off and on for three days. Wow! That really aided in healing my injuries. I even drank some of the sulfur water, and it seemed to help heal my digestive tract."

"That's very interesting," Sonny said.

"We've heard some of the old people in Anaktuvuk talk about that one, but it's so remote and the terrain so rough that I've never been there."

"That reminds me," I replied,

"The one time I was in Anaktuvuk Pass was when my friend and I had to land there for fuel several years ago. While there, we walked a short distance to the airport café or kitchen or something like that. Anyway, we sat at a long table, very tired, bleary-eyed and hungry.

An Eskimo lady came out and poured us hot coffee, for which we thanked her quite sincerely. Within minutes, she came back out with two big bowls of the best stew I've ever eaten. We tried to pay her, but she refused. When we asked what was in the pottage, she simply smiled and said, 'First caribou.'

We found out from the fuel guy that a boy in the village had taken his first caribou, and we just happened to get in on the celebration. We thanked her again and again. She just smiled real big. I've never forgotten her kindness to us nor how awesome that caribou stew tasted on a very cold, wet, windy day."

As I recounted this story, Sonny's face lit up like a two-mantle lantern.

"That was my mom!" he exclaimed proudly. She runs the airport kitchen, and, yes, she makes the best soups and stews anywhere in the Arctic. Everyone who has tried her cookin' says the same. I can't believe you actually met my mother. What are the chances?!"

Then, he looked at the floor and said quietly, "She passed away couple years ago."

"I'm sorry to hear that, Sonny. But, just so you know, my pilot friend and I could tell, just in that brief encounter, there was something genuine about her. She had a real presence and a lot of respect in that place."

My new friend beamed.

This providential coincidence instantly brought the three of us together like nothing else could have. The fact that I had met Sonny's mother and had shown appreciation for her cooking and complimented her character built a bridge between Sonny, Daniel, and me that otherwise would never have happened.

Little did I realize back then the significance that brief stop in Anaktuvuk Pass would have years later. But God did.

And little did I realize that very soon, God's sovereign hand would become even more visible.

I chanced a glance at Daniel. He was all smiles upon hearing I had met his grandma and loved her cooking.

I wanted very badly to talk more, but by this time, I was so exhausted, I couldn't keep my eyes open. For the past week, I had shivered more than slept and had almost starved to death. Now, enveloped by the warmth of a woodstove and with a full stomach, I was melting like bear fat over the fire.

"Sonny," I said, "would you and Daniel mind if I slept over here in the corner for a few hours? I'm afraid I'm gonna fall asleep right in the middle of our talk, and that'd be awful rude of me."

Sonny jumped to his feet and with great animation insisted I sleep in his bed, the lower bunk. He would take the upper bunk, and Daniel, the couch. Embarrassed but too tired to argue, I put my pack, bear poncho, and moose hide in the nearest corner.

As I was undressing down to my long johns, though, I got a nostril full of some wicked, animal odor. It was me. I smelled like spoiled meat, sour milk, and a garbage dump all combined!

Out in the giant, frozen wilderness, I hadn't realized just how horrific my body and foot odor had become. With the exception of the soak in the sulfuric hot springs months ago, I had not bathed in quite a while.

With a sheepish grin, I recalled the time soon after I was married that I came home after being out hunting for a week. I was so tired that I just undressed, crawled into bed, and fell sound asleep—but not for long. I was very quickly awakened by my wife. She was shaking me by the shoulders and saying,

"Wake up! Wake up! You are NOT getting in this bed without

taking a shower! You STINK!"

I could barely stay awake long enough to bathe. Once I did, however, and crawled back into bed, my wife said,

"Thank you, Mr. Pig!" and we fell asleep chuckling.

Here though, amongst new friends in their small cabin, I was embarrassed by the stench.

"Hey Sonny?"

"Yes," he replied.

"Would it be asking too much for you to heat up some water, give me a rag, and let me take a sponge bath in the dark? I really stink!"

They both laughed heartily.

"Me and Daniel were just sittin' here thinkin' the same thing," he replied, "I'll donate a bar of soap too!"

And we all had another good laugh.

— 19 —
THE COMFORT

"Hey, Bruce!" Someone far down the valley was calling my name. "Bru-u-uuce!"

The sound echoed for a long time, then, I awoke with a start. Sonny was shaking me. I sat up and said groggily,

"What? What's wrong!?"

"Nothing's wrong, man, but you've been asleep for twenty-one hours. Me and Daniel are just makin' sure you're alive."

"Yeah, I'm O.K," I groaned. "Actually, I'm *really* O.K. I haven't slept like that for months."

"Well, you're about to feel even better 'cause I just made a pot of fresh java and a stack of sourdough[17] blueberry pancakes."

I've never jumped out of bed as fast as I did that morning. The coffee would've been enough to lure me, but the promise of sourdough blueberry pancakes flipped my switch! I knew I was in for a tremendous taste-bud experience. To make the pancakes even better, they were lightly fried with a smidgen of bear grease.

Sonny placed three big ones, still steaming, on my plate and then handed me a dish of butter. I put a dollop on the top one and in between the others. Then I poured syrup all over them and cut a giant tri-layered bite. It barely fit in my mouth, and I have a fairly good-sized "pie hole."

Sonny's coffee was the perfect complement to offset the sweet syrup. About halfway through that stack, I stopped and said,

"Lord, if this is a dream, please don't let me wake up!"

Upon hearing this, Sonny and Daniel laughed, but I did not. I was

---

[17] Sourdough has a unique, sour accent to it like the name suggests. Many people in Alaska, natives included, have preserved a bit of sourdough starter in their family for many years. On special occasions, they draw just enough from the stash to ferment the rest of the dough. It makes some very delicious breads, donuts, and pancakes.

quite sincere.

"Your coffee is good and strong, like it should be. I despise weak coffee. It isn't bravado or an attempt to appear manly or to intimidate others; it's just common sense. The less coffee grounds there are, the less the water can absorb the taste of the coffee. Instead, all you get is the surface bitterness of the bean. With the proper amount of grounds, the hot water has more time to pick up the flavor as it passes through, making its way into the beaker or the pot."

"Well, I didn't know all the science involved," Sonny replied. "I just like it strong. Now I know why."

"The amount stays the same even if you have to put the grounds directly into the water and boil it. If you do that, once it boils, you remove it from direct heat and let it sit about five minutes. Then you add a dash of snow or ice water and the grounds sink immediately to the bottom. That's called 'camp coffee.'"

"That's how I make it," he said and showed me the pot. He had a stainless steel coffee pot with no "guts."

"I know," I said, feeling a little guilty.

"I drank what you had on the stove then made and consumed almost a whole pot before you guys got here."

"Hey!" Sonny replied, grinning real big, "I thought the coffee tasted fresher than I expected it to after sittin' on the stove all day. That explains it!"

Making good coffee is an art and just as Sonny's mom was an artist with stews, so Sonny was an artist with coffee. I said as much and could tell he appreciated the compliment. As we all sat around the table, I held the cup of black gold in my hands, savoring the aroma, sipping it, reverently.

"Did I really sleep twenty-one hours?"

"Well," Sonny said, "you crawled into bed the second time, you know, after your sponge bath—for which we both thank you . . ."

Upon hearing this, we all burst into laughter once again. Then Sonny continued,

"You crawled into bed at 7:00 p.m."

"What time is it now?" I asked.

"It's 4:30 p.m. We woke you up 'bout half hour ago."

"Man, I feel so refreshed!" I exclaimed.

"Thank you for letting me sleep. Thank you for everything. You both have been so kind. I hope someday to be able to repay you. For sure, I'll pay you for food and fuel."

"What fuel?" he queried.

"Uh, well," I stuttered, slightly embarrassed, "I'm sorry for sounding presumptuous, but I was hoping you might be willing to take me to the Haul Road so that I could hitchhike to Fairbanks."

At this request, Sonny sat back and rubbed his goatee thoughtfully.

"We'd be glad to run you to the highway, but it may not be the best way."

"Why not?" I questioned.

"Well," he said, gazing outside, "First off, if I did make a run for the highway, Daniel would have to stay here alone for a couple of days so as to lighten the load. He wouldn't be too fond of that idea.

Second, Its forty miles to the Dalton and I don't have enough fuel to do an extra eighty-mile turnaround.

Third, since we normally don't go past this cabin, we'd have to break trail, which could take a lot of time and fuel that we don't have.

Last, the opposite extreme is also quite possible: long stretches where there's no snow because of windstorms. That would create big problems for the snow machine, and if the temperature dropped, we'd really be in a fix!"

"Hey," I said, shaking my head and looking at the floor, "I'm at your mercy. I'm certainly in no position to argue. Besides, your reasoning sounds very convincing. If you want me to wait here at the cabin until you and Daniel can send help, I'm fine with that."

Sonny poured all three of us half a cup of coffee and then sat down and spoke:

"Since the trail back home is familiar to us and already broken in, we could leave a few things here, and you could ride on the snow machine with me."

"What about Daniel?" I queried.

"Daniel could ride in the gear sled. He's done it before. If it gets really cold, like -40 or worse, we got a couple of snow shelters already built. In other words, it'll be a heavy load and will take us a little more time to get to the village, but its way safer."

He continued, "Once we get to *our* home, you could fly to *your* home."

That last comment brought tears to my eyes, and I had to fight back some intense emotions. "Home," I whispered, lips quivering. I couldn't believe we were actually talking about home: MY home!

After I got my emotions under control, I responded,

"That sounds great, but the airfare from the villages to town is really high. I don't even have my wallet on me, much less any money."

At this, Sonny leaned forward and spoke in low but intense tones. Typically, most native peoples don't stare into your eyes, but Sonny was drilling a hole into mine.

"What transporter is gonna charge you a dime once they find out who you are and what happened to you? They're gonna be scramblin' to help the man who came back from the dead."

My brow wrinkled with uncertainty. He leaned back, sighed loudly and said,

"You don't have a clue do you?"

"About what?" I said, rather frustrated.

"Man, you and your friend have been in the news for months! They searched all over this huge state for you guys, but you didn't file a flight plan, and they never got a signal from your emergency locator. After a few weeks, they gave you guys up for dead. When you suddenly appear out of nowhere, the whole country is gonna go crazy. Man, the media people are gonna clean up on this one!" Then Sonny leaned forward so close I could smell his coffee breath. "Bruce," he said firmly, "you're gonna be a legend in less than a week."

I hadn't thought all this through.

"But," I said in frustration, "I couldn't care less about becoming a legend. That'll all die down after a while. All I care about is seeing my family again. I love and miss them so much it hurts!"

Upon hearing this last statement, Daniel suddenly got up, grabbed his parka and went outside.

I gave Sonny an inquisitive look. After a long silence, he spoke,

"Don't tell him I said nothin', but Daniel lost his mother just a few weeks ago. She was diagnosed with cancer last spring. It was so much through her body that the doctors said she had just three months, but she lived eight months. We had been separated for a while, but once she got the bad news, I moved back in with her. Soon after, we reconciled, and Daniel and I took care of her till the end. I'm so glad we made up before she . . . before she . . . went to heaven . . . if there is a heaven."

Upon hearing Sonny's last hesitant expression, I spoke very carefully, choosing every word:

"Sonny, I can tell you, there is a heaven, and it's a real and beautiful place."

"I wish I could know that for sure," he replied.

I waited, nervous about saying just the right thing. Silently, I asked God for help and wisdom. This man and his son had been through a lot of pain and grief, far more than I had. The last thing I wanted to do was tread upon their personal feelings and be offensive when they had done so much for me.

Finally, I spoke with a mixture of compassion and caution.

"May I ask you a couple of personal questions?"

"Sure," he said, "but if Daniel comes in . . ."

"Yep," I interrupted. "I'll change the subject real fast."

He nodded the go-ahead, so I began:

"Why do you believe, yet seem to doubt, that your wife is in heaven?"

"I believe it because I want to and because Daniel believes it. Also, Emily, my wife, was a woman of faith. That's actually one thing that drove us apart. I like to party, to drink, and have fun. She did too 'till she got religion. After that, she wouldn't party with me anymore, so I found someone else who would."

His eyes dropped.

I waited a minute and then said, "What do you mean, 'she got religion'?"

"Well," he said, "two years ago…this month actually…she confided in a friend of hers that she was very depressed and empty and had been thinking about suicide. Her friend, one of the elder ladies in the village who we call Grandma Mary, told her to read the Gospel of John in the Bible and they would talk about it. Well, a few days went by, and Emily went to Grandma Mary's house. They spent almost the whole day talkin.' When she came home, she was very different."

"How so?" I asked.

"She said that she had believed in Jesus Christ. I said, 'So do I. Doesn't everybody?'

She said, 'this is different, Sonny. Jesus saved me from my sins.'

"Well, I got kinda angry and told her she didn't have any sins; only I had sins—and I didn't need savin'!

She started talking about sacrifice and payment for sin and Jesus dying. It sounded crazy to me."

I responded:

"Emma was right on, Sonny. We all have offended God with our sins. The bible tells us in John 3:18 that we all need to be saved from the curse that hangs over us because of our sins. Jesus Christ, God's only begotten Son, offered Himself as a sacrifice on the cross and literally absorbed the curse of sin for us. He died that we might live. You see, God is holy. God is just. He must punish sin. But God is also love. He so loved the world—you, Daniel, Emma, me, every-body—that He took our punishment for us. *God died for us.*"

Sonny was quiet for a time. Then he continued his story:

"Well, I didn't understand. Can't say I do now either. In my frus-tration I said to her,

'Woman, you sound like a preacher! Please go outside, turn around, and come back in like you were before!' Then, I laughed in her face. But what she said next really got my attention. She said,

'I never wanna go back to what I was before, Sonny. I was very close to taking my own life. The weight of my guilt and the misery of having an empty soul was becoming more than I could carry. But now, I feel as though a great load has been lifted from my heart. For the first time in my life, I know that I am right with God and I belong to Him, and I am free from the guilt of my sins!'

"'O.K., well, good for you, Em, but that's not for me,' I snapped back.

'It is for you, Sonny, and deep down inside you know it's what you need. You don't need more alcohol or more parties, you need to become a child of God,' she said.

"Once I heard that, Bruce, I was out of words, so I just walked out and slammed the door behind me. I never let her talk to me about it again 'till she got cancer. Once we found out she was gonna die, I started treating her like I should've been treatin' her all along. Now, I'm tortured by the memories of my failures."

"How did Daniel respond?" I asked.

"Oh, he really didn't understand the gravity of it all until her last couple of days. He and his mom were very, very close. That's why he's still hurtin' and can't talk about it yet."

"Wow," I replied, "that's got to be tough on a ten-year-old."

"Yep," he responded, eyes to the floor.

"Well, here's the truth, Sonny," I said, holding my little New Testament in my hand.

"Even though I only have the New Testament with me right now, the entire Bible—both Old and New Testaments—is God's inspired Word. Your dear wife, Emily, was led to Grandma Mary by the providential hand of God so that she could hear the gospel and be saved from her sins and, ultimately, from being eternally separated from God."

"Do you believe Emily's in heaven?" Sonny asked, with wrinkled brow.

"Based on what you just told me and based on what the Bible says, absolutely."

"Where do you think I'm gonna go when I die?" he challenged.

"That depends on what you do with the truth God is giving to you right now and has been giving to you for quite some time, it sounds like."

His eyes filled with tears.

"I really mocked her, Bruce, and now it hurts me to think about it."

"I'm so sorry," I said. We sat in silence for a few minutes.

Then I continued: "I shouldn't ask so many questions, but I think I can help you deal with this."

"That's nice of you to say, but I don't think you can," he replied.

"Sometimes the guilt is so heavy I just start drinkin' till I pass out. At least it gives me some relief. Daniel begged me not to bring no liquor on this trip, so I didn't, but, man oh man, I wish I had!"

"Sonny," I said, "May I show you what Grandma Mary showed

Emily and what Emily was trying to tell you?"

"That'd be O.K.," he responded, "but how do you know what Grandma Mary told my wife?"

"I have a pretty good idea it came from the Gospel of John," I answered.

"O.K., go for it . . . but," Sonny reminded me, "if my boy comes in, feel free to keep talkin', Just don't mention his mom."

"Got it," I said and opened my New Testament to John 1:1-3.

After reading the passage, I explained to Sonny that Christ is the Son of God and is eternal and separate from creation just as God the Father is. I then turned to John 8 and explained how, when Jesus claimed to be equal with God in front of the religious crowd of His day, they became very angry and tried to stone Him to death. They knew exactly what Christ was saying and who He claimed to be. It was in the midst of this heated discussion that Jesus plainly told the most religious, self-righteous people of His day,

"If you do not believe that I am He, (Messiah/Savior) you will die in your sins [John 8:24]."

Then I said, "In other words, when God reveals to someone who Christ is and that person rejects the truth and dies in that condition of unbelief, he has no hope of salvation, no hope of forgiveness before God because Jesus Christ is God the Father's ONLY begotten Son [John 3:16]. There is no 'plan B' with God. It is either Christ or eternal separation from God" [Revelation 20:10-15].

Upon hearing this, Sonny responded:

"I thought that all religious people believe in Jesus."

I closed the New Testament and continued:

"Religious people today, for the most part, believe Jesus was a good man or a prophet or even a deity. But most religions today refuse to believe or teach that the forgiveness of our sins, the salvation of our souls, is in *Christ alone* and that *Christ alone* is Lord of all.

Most religious denominations in the world today teach a system of good works that serve as a kind of 'stairway to heaven.' Not only is this *not* taught in God's Word, but the Bible actually speaks against it very strongly.

Ephesians 2:8-9 is just one of many passages in God's Word that declare that man cannot save himself. It says,

'For by grace you have been saved through faith, and that not of yourselves; it is the gift of God, *not of works*, lest anyone should boast.'"

"So," Sonny interjected, "if Emily wasn't just being a religious nut, I *really* misunderstood!"

He looked down at the floor again, only this time, a tear followed his gaze.

"It's all right, Sonny. God understands. The Bible says, 'The natural man [the unsaved man] does not receive the things of the Spirit of God, for they are foolishness to him; nor can he know them, because they are spiritually discerned'" [1 Cor. 2:14].

"Yes," he replied, "but do you think Emily realized that I didn't understand?"

"She does now," I spoke softly.

At this, he looked up and smiled, nodding in agreement.

— 20 —
The Conversion

Suddenly, the door swung open and Daniel walked in, fresh snow on his fur hat and parka.

He held three ruffed grouse in his hand. When he saw us sitting on the couch, me with the Bible, Sonny with a tear halfway down his face, he turned to go back outside.

"Wait!" Sonny spoke quickly. "We're just talkin' Bible stuff. Come back in, Son; this stuff is good for both of us. Bruce here is givin' me a lot of good answers to questions I've had for a long time."

Upon hearing this, Daniel tossed the birds in the arctic entryway, set the .22 in the corner, and closed the door. He removed his parka and boots and sat on the bunk, off to the side. His cheeks were bright red from the cold, but his eyes were wide with . . . was it curiosity or was he excited to hear his dad talk so positively about the Bible? or was it simply the fact that he just shot three grouse?

Regardless, I jumped back into the conversation:

"So, as I was saying before Daniel came in . . . with dinner," I said, smiling,

"Jesus was more than a good man, more than a prophet, even more than a deity. He was (and is) the Eternal Son of God, the Lord of all creation. He is called the Son of God because He bears the exact nature, qualities, and sinless perfection as God does. He also had no beginning, just as God the Father had no beginning. He is also called Son of God because He is one with the Father, bears perfectly the image of the Father, and came to the earth from the Father, by means of the Holy Spirit.

In addition, Christ is the fulfillment of every Old Testament messianic prophecy. He is the Jewish Messiah as well as the Savior of the world. He is Lord of both Jew and Gentile."

I paused to determine whether Sonny was following me. He was looking at me intently, so I continued.

"He died on the cross, not by accident. It didn't surprise God the Father when Jesus was crucified. As a matter of fact, the Bible plainly states that the plan for the salvation of sinful, fallen man was already in the mind of God 'before the foundation of the world' [Eph. 1:4].

This plan involved the virgin birth of Christ, His sinless life, His agonizing crucifixion, and His literal resurrection from the grave. His bodily resurrection is the very heart of the gospel, yet most religions, including some that call themselves Christian, deny the literal, bodily resurrection of Jesus by redefining it or spiritualizing it or outright denouncing it."

With compassion, I looked at each of them.

"Sonny, Daniel, apart from trusting in the death, burial, and bodily resurrection of the Lord Jesus Christ for our soul's salvation, you have no hope of being right with God or of possessing eternal life.

The apostles of the early church plainly and boldly declared a message for which all of them were killed: 'There is no other name under heaven given among men by which we must be saved' [Acts 4:12].

Again, the Apostle Paul boldly wrote: 'If you confess with your mouth the Lord Jesus and believe in your heart that God has raised Him from the dead, you will be saved' [Rom. 10:9].

"In other words," I continued, "those who put their trust in His death, burial, and bodily resurrection, turning in their heart from sin to Christ, are *at that very moment* forgiven of all their sins, declared righteous in the presence of God, indwelt by the Holy Spirit, and given a brand new nature that makes them a new person.

The New Testament says: 'If anyone is in Christ, he is a new creation; old things are passed away; behold, all things have become new'" [2 Cor. 5:14].

Upon hearing this, Sonny spoke excitedly. "That explains what happened to my wife!"

Suddenly, we both stopped breathing and looked at Daniel.

"Sorry, Danny," Sonny said to him, "I know you still don't like to talk about her. I know it hurts."

"It's O.K., Dad," he whispered, slightly embarrassed. "I like hearing about this stuff."

Sonny's jaw dropped and his eyebrows went straight up.

"So," I continued, "getting back to the Gospel of John, we read in chapter three of a very religious man named Nicodemus who came looking for Jesus. He approached Jesus at night because he was afraid of getting into big trouble with his very religious friends who hated Christ."

Daniel surprised us by interrupting:

"Why did so many religious people hate Jesus?"

Sonny and I looked at each other and smiled, just slightly.

"Well, Daniel, the things that Jesus was teaching and the authority with which he spoke threatened the religious power structure of His day. The bottom line is that the true gospel—that is, the gospel that declares that anyone can be saved from the curse of sin and the power of death by trusting in the death, burial, and resurrection of Jesus—sets people free. However, false religions and false gospels enslave people to man-made organizations. So when the leaders of false religions feel threatened, they try to shut the proclaimers of the gospel up by intimidation or imprisonment or even by killing them. Some of the apostles themselves were martyred for refusing to stop preaching the gospel. Hundreds of thousands of martyrs have followed in their steps down through history.

So, understandably, Nicodemus was afraid of what his peers might think if they found out he was actually listening to the teachings of Christ. Therefore, he came to see Jesus at night and when he found Jesus, Nicodemus said,

'…We know that You are a teacher come from God; for no one can do these signs that You do unless God is with him' [John 3:2]. Well, Jesus got right to the point and responded,

'Unless one is born again, he cannot see the kingdom of God' [John 3:3].

"This statement really got Nic's attention. Since he knew only of the physical birth, when we come out of our mother's womb as babies, he was confused and said,

'How can a man be born when he is old? Can he enter the second time into his mother's womb and be born?' [John 3:4]. Jesus clarified His statement and said,

'That which is born of the flesh is flesh, and that which is born of

171

the Spirit is spirit' [John 3:6].

In other words, you must be born of water (our first birth) and of the spirit (our second birth)."

"So is it bad to go to church?" Daniel asked, obviously still thinking about my comments on religion.

"No, absolutely not. But no church or religious organization can save you from your sins. That is something only Christ has the power to do. The right kind of church will always point people to Christ for salvation, not to their organization and not to a system of good works."

"This is really startin' to sound familiar, Bruce," Sonny declared excitedly.

"This is the kinda stuff Emily tried to talk to me 'bout after her visits with Grandma Mary. Only now, instead of makin' fun of it, I'm startin' to understand it!"

"So, it's O.K. with you guys if I continue? I asked.

"I'm all ears… that is, if Daniel doesn't mind."

"I wanna hear it, too," Daniel said. "It kinda feels like Mom is here with us. This is what she talked to me about the . . . the last couple of days," Daniel said. Then he was silent again.

"O.K. then," Sonny replied, "if you say it's all right, I'd like to hear more, 'cause I always thought your mom just got fooled by a bunch of religious fanatics. But I'm startin' to see that I was wrong—really wrong."

Daniel nodded his approval.

"It's fine, Dad, even though it kinda hurts, but it kinda makes me feel good at the same time. It's hard to explain."

"Bruce," said Sonny, "we've never had anyone say it like you just did. I feel like I understand it for the first time."

"Maybe you just listened for the first time," I said respectfully.

"Why did my mom have to die?" Daniel blurted out. His eyes filled with tears and he quickly avoided my gaze.

"That's a great question, Daniel," I responded.

"As a matter of fact, that is probably the most asked question about God: If God is so good, why is there evil and suffering and death everywhere? Why doesn't God rescue all of us from pain and death, *right now*?"

"Exactly!" Sonny almost shouted. "I been wantin' to ask that but didn't know how to put it. Thanks for bringin' that up, Dan-boy."

"The truth is, God *has* rescued us," I said.

"The Bible tells us that in the very beginning, God gave Adam and Eve one command: 'Of the tree of the knowledge of good and evil you shall not eat, for in the day that you eat of it you shall surely die' [Gen. 2:17]. Well, by that time, Satan had already rebelled against God and been cast out of heaven [Isaiah 14]. Since that time, his goal, his passion, has been to ruin everything God does in order to rob God of His glory."

Sonny and Daniel were listening with rapt attention.

"So," I continued, "when God created man, Satan saw an opportunity to thwart God's plan, ruin His creation, and put his creator to shame. That's why he tempted Eve to disobey God by persuading her to eat the now infamous forbidden fruit. Eve did so and then convinced Adam to sin against God. Mankind has been sinning and running from God ever since.

God confronted Adam with his disobedience, pronounced judgment on Satan, Eve, and, finally, Adam [Gen. 3:1-19]. That is why we die, Daniel.

The Bible says in Romans 5:12, 'Just as through one man [Adam] sin entered into the world, and death through sin, and thus death spread through all men, because all sinned.'

But guess what?"

"What?" they said in unison.

"None of this took God by surprise. Remember what I alluded to a few minutes ago: The Bible says in several places that Christ was offered as a sacrifice for our sins, from 'before the foundation of the world.' Now, I'd like to actually show you guys where in Scripture that is stated."

I then read Ephesians 1:3-4, 1 Peter 1:18-20, and Revelation 13:8 from my New Testament.

"In other words, God has a plan; it existed before creation and can never be derailed. God is all-powerful and all-knowing. He is sovereign. The fact that His plan is still unfolding and that the world is still a place of sin and death doesn't mean God doesn't care or that He is powerless. On the contrary, the existence of death, pain, suffering, and sorrow only serve to illustrate that God's Word is true and God's promise cannot be broken."

"Then what's he waiting for?" Daniel asked. "Why does God wait? Why doesn't He just kill Satan now and give me my mother back?"

"Those are great questions, Dan-man, and the Bible has the answer.

In 2 Peter 3: 9 God's Word says, 'The Lord is not slack [irresponsible] concerning His promise, as some count slackness [tardiness], but is longsuffering toward us, not willing that any should perish but that all should come to repentance.'"

"What does that mean?" Daniel asked with wrinkled brow.

"Well, it means that God patiently waits for more souls to repent of sin and believe in His Son, Jesus Christ. Every day, thousands of people around the world turn to Christ and are saved from the holy wrath of God by embracing the loving gift of God.

Romans 6:23 says, 'The wages of sin is death, but the gift of God is eternal life in Christ Jesus our Lord.'"

I could tell Sonny was getting it but not Daniel.

"Let me put it this way, Daniel: what if God had said ten years ago, 'Enough already! I am going to end all things *now*!' Would your mom have had the opportunity to talk to Grandma Mary and become a child of God?"

"No," Daniel replied thoughtfully.

"What if God had said 'enough!' just six months ago, Daniel? Did you know how to believe in Jesus just six months ago?"

"No." he said.

"And," I continued, "We wouldn't be having this talk together . . ."

"And there'd be no hope for *me* either," Sonny mumbled.

"So, guys, you see, sin and death and sorrow still exist in the world, not because God enjoys watching people suffer or because He doesn't care or because He is powerless, but because the curse of sin will end when He says the time is right. At the perfect time, the door of salvation will close, and the fires of judgment will fall. But until then, our gracious God invites everyone, everywhere, to repent and be saved."

"So . . . is *that* what Emily did?" Sonny asked intently.

His question, though meek, was powerful. I knew this was a crucial time, not just in our conversation, but in Sonny's life. I hesitated and silently prayed for wisdom before answering him.

"Yes, Sonny, it sounds to me like that is exactly what your wife did and, quite frankly, you should respond the same way, the way the Bible says we all should respond when we hear the gospel.

Acts 16:31 says, 'Believe on the Lord Jesus Christ, and you will be saved.'

And Romans 10:13 says, 'Whoever calls on the name of the Lord shall be saved.'"

There was a full minute of very uncomfortable silence in that little cabin. The coals in the stove were quietly sizzling. The moment just seemed too fragile for me to say anything more. I had explained the gospel to this grieving father and son the best I knew how. I had tried to back up everything I told them with the Bible, in its context. I had done my best not to manipulate these dear people.

Now, the rest was up to the Holy Spirit of God.

Sonny's head was down, his arms resting on his knees, hands folded.

Daniel was leaning all the way back on the couch, looking at his hands.

Suddenly, Sonny broke the silence.

"I'm ready," he declared.

My heart was in my throat. This man, weary with the burdens of sin and grief, had just made the most important decision of his life.

"If you are ready to take that step of faith, turning in your soul from sin to Christ, Sonny, I'm here to encourage you, but I cannot believe for you or call out to God for you. You must do that yourself. Most importantly, repentance and faith are things the Holy Spirit of God puts in your heart. Prayer is simply an outward expression of what has very likely already taken place inside your soul."

Slowly, I slid off the chair and turned to get on my knees. Sonny did the same. I figured Daniel stayed put because I didn't hear anything from where he sat.

"I don't know…how to…pray," Sonny said, voice breaking.

"There is no formal set of words, no prescribed prayer, Sonny. Just tell God what's going on right now in your soul. Admit your sinful, helpless condition and confess Jesus as your Lord and Savior."

There was a moment of silence and then a sound more beautiful than the song of a thousand angels . . .

"God . . ." Sonny said; then he lost it. Sonny just fell apart kneeling there beside me.

Suddenly, I heard Daniel rush over to his dad. I chanced a peek.

They were kneeling, side-by-side. Daniel's arm was as far around his dad's shoulders as he could reach.

"God," Sonny continued, sobbing.

"I been fightin' You a long time. I treated You like . . . an enemy. I didn't Know You were my Friend all this time. I'm really, really sorry. I am a sinful man. I've done lots of bad things my whole life. Please forgive me. I love Jesus, and I believe in Him. Please save me like you did Emily. I wanna be cleaned up."

At this, both Sonny and Daniel clung to each other and cried together for quite a while.

After some time, things settled down. They arose at the same time and sat on the couch, hands held tightly, both wiping the tears away.

I made it a point to look down just out of respect for their privacy at such an emotional time. I started to grab my griz hide and go outside, but then Sonny spoke.

"What about you, Dan?" he said quietly. "You gonna believe in Jesus with me?"

"I did," Daniel replied.

Once again, Sonny's eyebrows shot straight up.

"Really? Just now?"

I felt awkward, listening to this private talk between father and son, but I really needed to know what Daniel was thinking and what he was trying to tell his dad. So I held my breath and tried to be a lot smaller in that moment.

"No," Daniel answered. "I prayed to God back in the summer. I went to check on Mom one morning and she motioned for me to come closer. I did, and she whispered something out of that book of John in my ear. I knelt beside her, and she said to me some of the stuff Bruce just said, and I prayed to God and we cried together just like you and me did right now."

"Wow!" Sonny exclaimed. "Why didn't you tell me?"

Daniel hesitated, nervously wringing his hands, and then said, "I was afraid you would yell at me."

Upon hearing this, Sonny grabbed his boy, and they both started crying all over again.

I could hear Daniel's muffled voice as he buried his head in his dad's shoulder:

"I been prayin' for you, Dad!" he cried. "God brought us here to this cabin and brought this man out of nowhere and answered my prayer!"

Upon hearing this, I was stunned—absolutely stunned.

"Oh, my!" I exclaimed, under my breath. "Out of the mouth of babes." [Psalm 8:2].

In one sentence, this ten-year-old boy had given me the explanation for which I had been searching this entire journey. The truth of it all struck my soul like lightening! Everything that had happened over the past five months started to make sense:

The crash, the cave, the agonizing delays, the arduous journey, the protection, the provision—every storm, every frustration, every coincidence, every miracle—all of it really started to come into focus.

"Our God really is in control!" I said out loud, with trembling voice. Suddenly, I stood.

"Had I arrived here just a day or two earlier or later, we likely would've never crossed paths."

Upon realizing all God had done to answer the prayer of a ten-year-old boy in a remote Arctic village, I rushed over to the couch and we all hugged and cried and prayed and thanked our great God together!

— 21 —
THE CONCLUSION

Later that night, as we were eating the grouse Daniel had taken, I remembered something he had said. I asked,

"Daniel, do you recall the verse out of the Gospel of John that your mom whispered in your ear just before you prayed and asked the Lord to save you?"

"Not all of it," he replied "but it was something like 'Don't let your heart be troubled.'"

"Oh, yes," I said, restraining my excitement. "That's a wonderful passage, full of promise."

"How come?" he asked.

"Those verses are found in John 14. Jesus was explaining to His disciples that He was about to go to Jerusalem and give His life for the sins of the world. They weren't quite sure what He meant at the time, but it worried them, even made them fearful.

Actually, Jesus was comforting and reassuring them when he said, 'Let not your heart be troubled; you believe in God, believe also in Me. In My Father's house [heaven] are many mansions [resting places]; . . . I go to prepare a place for you. And if I go and prepare a place for you, I will come again and receive you to Myself; that where I am, there you may be also. And where I go you know, and the way you know. Thomas said to Him, Lord, we know not where you are going, and how can we know the way? Jesus said to him, I am the way, the truth, and the life. No one comes to the Father except through Me.'"

"Daniel, I have no doubt that your mother shared those Bible verses with you to plant at least two great truths in your heart:

"First, she very likely wanted you to be comforted by knowing Jesus had prepared a place for her in heaven and that she would be just fine.

Second, your mother was telling you, once more, that Jesus is the only way to heaven."

I paused and then asked,

"Is that when you and your mom prayed together and you actually trusted Christ to save you from your sins?"

"Yes," Daniel replied firmly, his black eyes held fast to mine.

"That's awesome." I responded. "That is just awesome that your sweet mother gave you such a great gift—the greatest gift, as a matter of fact—before her soul entered into the presence of the Lord!"

Upon hearing that, the moment became even more unforgettable when Daniel got up, walked around the table, and extended his hand to me. Curious but flattered, I shook his hand lightly, remembering that Alaska natives don't shake hands vigorously like many other people do.

Then he said,

"You and me . . . we are like family because you were kind to my great-grandma, and… we both believe in Jesus." I was thrilled out of my gourd, to put it mildly.

"I agree!" Sonny exclaimed. "I agree totally with what my boy says!"

Smiling as big as one of Sonny's pancakes I said:

"Our love for family makes us friends, our faith in Christ makes us family."

"So does that mean you're gonna call me 'Uncle Bruce' from now on?" I asked Daniel, smiling.

"Yep," he replied and hugged me as big and strong as any ten year old could.

Once we pushed back from the table, full of grouse and coffee in hand, I ventured the big question:

"O.K., so… When can we leave for Anaktuvuk?"

Scratching his chin thoughtfully, Sonny replied, "How 'bout in the morning, we get up 'bout six, eat a good breakfast—"

"With coffee?" I interrupted.

"Yes, of course, with gallons of coffee," Sonny said, chuckling.

"Then," he continued, "we unload our trapping box and a few other things from the machine, fuel up, including a couple five-gallon cans, pack some food, and hit the trail . . . weather permitting."

"Weather permitting?" I asked, with a note of concern.

"Yes, it's gotta be warmer than -30 with no strong winds, or I won't venture out from the cabin. It's too easy for the machine to break down in extreme cold and if the wind is blowing strong, we can't see the trail or any landmarks."

Immediately, I walked to the window and looked outside. There was no wind. The thermometer read -22. I prayed the weather would do nothing but improve.

That night, it was a very long time before I fell asleep. The abundance of rest, the good food, the coffee, and, most of all, the awesome experience of God's sovereign hand bringing me and Sonny and Daniel together…all of these things combined had me wired… not to mention the excitement generated from the realization that I would soon be reunited with my family!

I tossed and turned most of the night.

Finally, sleep descended upon me, heavily. I didn't even hear Sonny's watch alarm when it beeped.

What actually did wake me was the "Clang! Clang! Clang!" when Sonny dropped the frying pan on the floor. I guessed that was my good morning wake-up call and I was happy to hear it.

I swung my feet to the floor and shouted, "coffee time!"

Sonny was busy cookin' and grinnin'. Daniel didn't move. It did not matter. I was up, dressed, and almost running in place by the time the coffee was brewing.

I sprinted to the window with my flashlight and looked outside. It was -20 and there was no wind.

"Awesome! It looks like we can start for home today. By the time the sun rises, it might even warm up a little. C'mon, Daniel," I coaxed, "let's get crackin'!"

"C'mon, Daniel," Sonny teased. "This guy ain't gonna leave us alone when he's so close to home. We might as well have some breakfast and load up."

I felt like a kid on Christmas morning.

It took Daniel about thirty minutes to start feeling that way, but he eventually got some coffee in his blood and started getting excited too. He said he wanted to show me off to all his buddies in the village.

"Careful now," I said, "I ain't some kinda moose dropping souvenir you found out on the trail, ya know."

At this, he just grinned and gave me a good morning hug, complete with morning breath.

By nine o'clock, we were loaded up, snow machine idling, ready for takeoff.

Sonny had a black and yellow Ski-doo trapper's machine with a low windshield, extended track, and room for a second passenger to sit behind the driver. This kind of machine is known as a two-up. He was towing a well-built trapper's sled in which he had secured my griz poncho, daypack, sleeping bag, and hatchet.

I had purposely left the blue tarp and the moose hide remnant at their cabin. They had trimmed down their gear dramatically except for some dried meat, a .30-.30 rifle, survival gear, and two five-gallon cans of extra fuel. Daniel was nestled in the middle of all our soft gear. He was decked out in all his native winter garb. I sat directly behind Sonny wearing the warm clothes they had given me, happy to be free from the griz hide.

Sonny started to press the throttle when suddenly I shouted, "Wait!"

He spun around. "You forget something in the cabin?" he yelled above the engine noise.

"No, but we should pray before leaving," I said loudly.

Instantly, they removed their fur trapper hats. I did as well and then surprised Sonny by asking him to pray for us.

Timidly at first, he began:

"Lord, we done this trip many times, me and Daniel, but this time . . . well, we know *You* now . . . and this time . . . it's different. Thanks for bringin' us a new friend to explain to us the way to You . . . and to Emily. I don't know how prayer works, but if possible, please tell Emily I'm part of Your family now and that we're gonna see each other again someday. Amen. Oh! And keep us safe. Amen…"

…Then Daniel chimed in:

"And help Uncle Bruce to get back home real soon. Amen again."

Our smiles and tears were nigh frozen but our hearts were aflame.

Sonny pushed in the throttle, and I was quickly on my way to freedom and family.

"Home—our destination! God—our destiny!" I shouted. Both fists raised to the sky.

If you made any kind of a spiritual decision while reading this book, please contact me via my website **www.godofthebrooks.com** so that I can encourage you and provide you with the tools you need to continue your walk with God.